YOURS:

Billionaire CEO Romance
(Yours to Take, Yours to Teach, Yours to Keep)

Cathryn Fox

Yours To Take

One

"Please tell me you're not serious?"

Jaw slack, and hands planted on the small round table, Rebecca Andrews stared at her three best friends, hardly able to believe what they were suggesting.

Lilliana James closed her palm over Rebecca's hand and gave a reassuring squeeze. Even though the lights had been dimmed in their favorite New York piano bar, a place where they all convened after a challenging day in the courtroom, Rebecca didn't miss the sympathy in her friend's big brown eyes when she said, "Come on, Becs, you know as well as I do that you need a vacation."

"It's not a vacation she needs," Melanie Collins piped in, running her fingers up and down the crystal stemware in a highly suggestive manner that had Rebecca's thoughts careening in an erotic direction.

She smirked and added, "What she needs is to get laid. Plain and simple."

"Good, God," Rebecca murmured under her breath, hoping like hell no one in the near vicinity could hear her tell-it-like-it-is friend.

"Don't even try to deny it," Melanie challenged playfully, her eyes gleaming with mischief.

As their conversation headed south—literally—Rebecca fished her olive out of the martini glass and gestured the bartender for another, having decided then and there that this was the perfect occasion to overturn her two two-drink rule. Hell, who could blame her for wanting to consume copious amounts of alcohol after discovering her well-meaning friends wanted to send her to some sort of sex club on a private island off the coast of Nova Scotia?

She chewed on her olive as her glance went to the tickets on the table—one for a resort called Freedom, the other for the private charter that was scheduled to fly her there first thing tomorrow. Groaning, she took in the other patrons seated around them, many of whom were colleagues, their identities masked by the lounge's dark lighting and intimate seating. She leaned forward, desperate to keep this embarrassing conversation private, and arched an accusing brow. "How long have you three been scheming this up, anyway?"

"Just a few weeks now," Melanie answered.

Rebecca did the mental math, her thoughts rewinding to three weeks ago, then shook her head, suddenly understanding what this was really all about. "Look, Jon didn't break up with me. I broke up with him." When her rebuttal was met with silence, she desperately searched for an alliance in the group. Her glance met Sophie's and she cast her a pleading look.

But Sophie simply shrugged and said, "Just like you broke up with Justin, Matthew, Phillip…"

"And we know, we know," Melanie said, rolling her eyes. "You just weren't compatible."

Rebecca held her hands up, palms out. "Okay, fine. I get it. You're saying I'm too picky." She frowned, and added, "It's just that…well, we weren't…they weren't," she paused, unable to put in to words what she truly felt. How could she explain what was missing from those relationships, when she couldn't identify it herself?

She took a moment to consider the men from her past. Not only were they successful, kind and generous, they were also deeply considerate lovers. A woman in her right mind would jump at the chance to date any one of those men. She sighed inwardly. Okay, perhaps the problem really did lie with her, and *she* was the one who wasn't in her right mind. But she just couldn't seem to find a man that suited her.

If only she could figure out what it was that was lacking…

Oddly enough her thoughts drifted back to last year's trial against Montgomery Charters, specifically to Quinn Montgomery, owner of the airline, and one of the world's youngest, self-made millionaires. Rebecca always prided herself on being calm, cool and collected, inside the courtroom and out, but there was just something about that man's steely command that threw her off her game. Whenever she met those intense black eyes from across the table, eyes that looked like they could see into the depth of her soul, something always compelled her to shy away. She wasn't sure what it was about the powerful tycoon that had her reacting in such a peculiar way, she only knew that he had the ability to rattle her hard-earned control, and because of it, she needed to keep her distance.

The bartender stepped up to the table with fresh drinks, and as his presence pulled her thoughts back to the conversation at hand, Rebecca shook her head, wondering why she was thinking of the powerful and enigmatic Quinn Montgomery after all this time.

Perhaps it was the fact that her friends had booked her flight through his airline...or perhaps it was something else entirely. Either way, he was a man she never wanted to come up against again, because the next time she wasn't so sure she could keep her composure.

"It's just a weekend away to relax, let you hair down." Melanie waved a dismissive hand like what they were suggesting was nothing more than an innocent day at the spa. Except what they wanted her to do had sex, sin and seduction written all over it. "Maybe at Freedom you'll learn to relax and stop trying to be in control of everything all the time."

Rebecca squared her shoulders and tucked a long, loose strand of hair back into the bun piled at the top of her head. "Hey, I don't always have to be in control of everything."

Her rebuttal was met with laughter. Okay, so maybe it was true, but it wasn't her fault. She'd come from nothing and had to work hard to get where she was, and it wasn't easy to loosen up and let go. Controlling every aspect of her life was how she got to where she was today.

And where is that, some inner voice asked, only to answer with, *alone every night, with nothing but a battery-operated friend to keep you warm.*

Sophie squeezed her hand and Rebecca looked up to meet a pair of big blue eyes full of genuine concern. "You've been so uptight that we just thought you could use a bit of time to yourself."

Melanie bobbed her head. "And you never know, while you're away maybe you'll figure out what it is you're looking for in a man."

"At a sex resort?"

"It's not a sex resort," Lilliana reassured her. "It's just a place where single people go to meet others."

Slipping into lawyer mode, Rebecca challenged, "But when you say *others*, you mean the opposite sex right? So in my book that's a sex resort." Rebecca picked up the ticket and turned it over in her hand, but as she thought about it, really, really thought about what her friend's were offering her, her body began warming in the most intimate places. She wet her suddenly dry lips, her nipples tightening as she envisioned the salacious activities that undoubtedly took place on the exclusive island.

A strange garbled noise caught in her throat and she shook her head to clear it. God, she must be crazy—and the jury was still out on that—because for a moment there she actually found herself considering their ludicrous offer.

Rebecca squinted to read the fine print. "Is this place even legal?"

"Of course it is, and you leave first thing in the morning." Melanie snatched the ticket and shoved it into Rebecca's purse; her way of saying the topic was no longer up for debate.

Rebecca stiffened. "I don't think—"

"Which is why we're doing the thinking for you," Lillian countered.

"If you're not at the airport by nine sharp, I'll personally drag you from your bed and take you there." Melanie finished her drink, and grinned. "And don't come back until you've had at least a dozen orgasms."

"And we don't want to hear a peep from you until Monday morning, when we'll meet you at the office to hear all the juicy details," Lilliana said. "If you call before then, we won't answer."

"That's right," Sophie added, pointing to Rebecca's purse. "You've just been gifted with a ticked to Freedom. So go. Be free."

* * *

Quinn Montgomery took one look at the flight manifest and felt his cock swell with an excitement he hadn't felt in a long time. As the Dom in him stirred to life, he carefully set the paper on his desk and took two measured steps to his office window. He adjusted his tie and blinked against the bright morning rays glistening on the wings of the Cessna idling quietly on the tarmac below. He turned his attention to his ground crew, who were performing maintenance checks before today's scheduled flights, but his thoughts were too preoccupied with the names on his manifest, one name in particular, to follow their progress.

Rebecca Andrews.

Now what were the odds that the lawyer who'd cost his company hundreds of thousands of dollars had booked a charter on one of his crafts? A charter to a hedonistic resort, nonetheless.

His mind raced back to last year's trial, and to the lawsuit Ms. Andrews' client never should have won. How it was his company's fault that Ms. Andrews' client had booked a package though a shady travel agent, only to find herself alone and stranded on Nantucket Island during one of the year's worst storm was beyond him. Yet in the end, his company had to go good for the damages, as well as the mental stress and loss of wages that the woman had allegedly suffered.

Quinn's mouth twitched and he scrubbed his hand over his chin as he rolled back and forth on the balls of his feet. While the money was only a drop in the bucket for his company, the tricks the lawyer had used to get what she wanted from him, left him wanting to use a few tricks of his own—to get what he wanted from her.

Oh yeah, watching her from the hot seat during his trial, watching that sharp tongue of hers in action, had him wanting to find other ways to put that smart mouth of hers to work. Heat prowled through his body as he thought about how Ms. Andrews kept her control close, kept her body poised and her head held high. But during the proceeding, every time her glance had landed on him and she lowered her gaze in a submissive move, he knew she was in denial. Damned if he didn't want to be the one to open her eyes and her body, and put her in touch with her deeper needs.

Even though they'd never crossed paths since the trial, she'd consumed his thoughts for well over a year now. He'd spent many nights thinking about the ways he'd like to strip her bare and give her ass a good hard paddling for wrongfully stealing money from his company. But the truth was, what he wanted had little to do with revenge, and more to do with showing the woman who dressed in prim and proper business suits that real control came in the form of surrender.

With his cock throbbing, and heat coursing through him, he moved back to his desk to look over the day's schedule a second time. He glanced at her name again, and his entire body came alive, because there was no denying that he'd just been gifted the perfect opportunity to help her free her submissive side. Of course, given that he'd only have one weekend, he'd have no choice but to push her limits and resort to some stronger methods to seduce the submission out of her. His fingers itched as he thought about that lush heart-shaped ass of hers and how much it needed his attention.

He inspected the itinerary closer and discovered that Jack Armstrong, a pilot that had been with the company since its early days was scheduled to depart for Freedom at nine sharp—Ms. Andrews the only passenger on board. Quinn considered her final destination. Not only had his company taken guests to the private island numerous time, he personally knew the resort well, having played there a time or two. Although this time he suspected the plane wasn't going to make it to the well-known island nestled in the Atlantic Ocean, especially if he was the one in the pilot seat.

He picked up the paper, and traced his finger over her name as a devious plan began to formulate in his mind. As he sorted through all the naughty details, all the tricks he was going to use on her, he checked his watch then picked up his phone to call his personal assistant. After giving her a list of things he needed before take-off, he dialed a friend and called in a favor. Once all the pieces were in place, and the discreet information he needed was on its way, he crossed Jack's name off the manifesto, shrugged out of his dress jacket and grabbed his flight suit. Ms. Andrews might be looking for a little adventure at Freedom, but he'd be damned if he wasn't going to be the guy to give her what she really wanted, yet had no idea how much she needed.

Two

Rebecca wrung her damp hands together and tried to wrestle her nerves into submission as the small plane cruised through the cloudless sky. It wasn't so much that she hated flying, it had more to do with what waited for her when they landed on the private island. But since her friends had gone to so much trouble to put this package together for her, and she truly didn't want to disappoint them, she couldn't very well say no and let it go to waste. Which was why she was currently flying over the Atlantic Ocean, on the way to some sordid sex club. That, of course, didn't mean she had to partake in any of the resort activities, whatever they might be.

She glanced at her suitcase, and relaxed a tiny bit, knowing her files were tucked safely inside. Maybe the weekend wouldn't be so bad after all. She could hole up in her room and get some work done and her friends would be none the wiser.

Pushing back into her seat, she looked at the ground below then stole a glance at the pilot negotiating the skies in front of her. He was a big man, with broad shoulders and a hard body—one that filled out his dark flight suit rather nicely thank you very much—and gave her something to think about other than her final destination. She perused his profile, but with his hat pulled low and pair of dark sunglasses covering his features, she couldn't identify his face. She studied him a moment longer, and felt a niggling in the depths of her stomach. There was just something about him that felt familiar—something that reminded her of Quinn Montgomery—but she knew it was well below the stature of a man who ran a multimillion-dollar company to be flying a customer to a sex resort.

She turned and stared out the window for the remainder of the trip and when the plane finally landed, she looked around, detailing the small island fringed by the cold waves of the Atlantic. The makeshift runway was surrounded by lush foliage, and off in the distance, high on a hill, she spotted an impressive estate. Although upon closer inspection, it looked more like a millionaire's summer home than a lavish resort where hedonist activities took place. And if this was a sex resort, where was everyone? The place was empty. Not a single vacationer to be found.

She leaned forward and tapped the pilot's shoulder, certain he'd made a mistake. But when he unbuckled his harness, opened the cockpit door and climbed from the plane, the niggling in her stomach grew to a full blown case of panic.

What is going on?

The pilot widened the door even more, and with every nerve in her body on edge, she remained seated. She straightened her back and said, "I think there's been a mistake."

"There's been no mistake."

Her heart jumped into her throat because the second he spoke, the second she heard that rich deep voice, one that evoked a myriad of sinful thoughts and had her mind whirling back to the trial of Quinn Montgomery, she knew her day had just gone from bad to worse.

"What's going on?" she demanded, steeling herself as alarm flashed through her.

Mr. Montgomery removed his hat and glasses, and when she caught the intensity in those shrewd, dark eyes, a fine shiver moved through her, and much to her dismay she found it most difficult to hold his steely gaze.

"Welcome to Montgomery estate," he said, his tone low, controlled as he opened his palm to her. "My summer home."

Refusing to accept the offered hand, she forced herself to level him with a stare and climbed from the plane on her own volition. Even though he was dressed in a flight suit, everything about his demeanor screamed of sex, sin, seduction…long hard spankings.

Okay, where the hell had that thought come from?

Exasperated with the way he could affect her without even trying, she fished her phone out of her purse and held it high. She checked for a signal, then cursed silently. Her mind raced to her friends and their final warning last night. Truthfully, even if her phone worked here in the middle of nowhere, she knew her calls would go unanswered.

Don't come home until you've had at least a dozen orgasms.

Without conscious thought her glance drifted to Mr. Montgomery's hands, and her mind took that second to think about what they'd feel like on her skin, touching her, stroking her, bringing her to orgasm again and again. Oh God! Her entire body flushed and there wasn't a damn thing she could do to stifle the tortured moan crawling out of her throat. Just standing next to a man who could undoubtedly divide and conquer with a simple look had her feeling edgy, out of control, completely at his mercy.

He took a measured step closer and as his presence dominated the wide expanse of island, and threw her off her game, she worked to summon a modicum of composure and asked in her best professional voice, "What do you want?"

He cocked his head, his glance leisurely moving over her face. "Relax, Ms. Andrews, you're not in the courtroom anymore." His smile came slow. "You don't get to ask the questions here."

Her towered over her, and with a stance that was both commanding and authoritative it became abundantly clear that here, on his private island, she was now playing in his territory, by his rules. No longer was she the one calling the shots.

Oddly enough, equal mixtures of excitement and apprehension trickled through her and elicited a shiver from deep within. What the hell was going on with her?

"I'm not going to hurt you if that's what you're worried about."

"I'm worried about a lot of things," she countered, shading the hot, morning sun from her eyes while trying to hide her reactions from him.

The muscles along his jaw flexed. "And that is why you're here, Ms. Andrews." Everything in the slow, calculated way he spoke did the most peculiar things to her libido.

Tension grew in her body and her thoughts raced to catch up. "What is that supposed to mean?"

Silence hung for a long time, her flesh growing hotter with each passing second, although she suspected it had little to do with the blinding rays beating down on her. "It's time to stop worrying and let someone take a few decisions out of your hands."

"Someone? Let me guess, that someone would be you?" she shot back.

Anticipation moved over his eyes when he answered with, "Of course."

She swallowed. "And how do you plan to do that?"

"You'll see," he said, the slow, promising way he drew out those two little words hinting at something wickedly intimate.

She sucked in a breath. "And what you're going to *see* is the inside of a prison, because this—" she paused to wave her arm around the isolated island "—this is kidnapping."

"Kidnapping?" He rocked on his feet like he was mulling that over. "I suppose if that's how you want to look at it, then yes, it's kidnapping." He held his hand out. "Now shall we?"

She jerked away from him. "Now, we shall not. You can take me back home right now." Folding her arms, she rooted her feet, refusing to budge.

The corner of his mouth twitched—*twitched*, like he was laughing at her. "Don't worry, Rebecca. I won't make you do anything you don't want to do."

Oh God, the rich, sensual way he said her name, the leisurely way it rolled off the tip of his tongue with such heat and hunger filled her with need and excited her in ways that didn't make sense, considering he'd just kidnapped her and planned to do God knows what to her.

I won't make you do anything you don't want to do.

His amusement vanished. "Now why don't you come inside, and have something cool to drink. You're flushed."

"It's hot."

He arched a brow, skepticism flashing in his black eyes. "Perhaps," he said.

Just then Rebecca spotted a middle-aged man coming their way, and her pulse leapt with hope. Maybe she could plead her case, tell him she was being held against her will, and he could call for help, get her off this isolated island. But when she glanced back at Quinn he had a knowing looking on his face.

"There are three *loyal* members of my staff here, and they answer to me only." He waved a hand. "That is Michael, and he's here to attend to your needs during your visit."

"What I need is to get out of here," she said flatly.

Ignoring her he continued, "You'll also meet Ester, my cook, and Mario, the grounds keeper."

Michael nodded his head and greeted them both, then proceeded to grab their luggage from the plane. "Right this way, ma'am," he said, gesturing toward the foliage lined path leading up to the grand estate.

Deciding to follow, and hoping there was a landline inside the house, she pushed past Mr. Montgomery and stayed close to Michael as he led the way. Once inside the opulent, airy home, the cool air conditioning refreshing against her hot skin, she searched for a phone.

As she panned the living space, she took in the huge floor-to-ceiling windows lining the back of the house, and the magnificent view of the ocean below. Michael disappeared up the wide staircase with their luggage in tow, and Rebecca stepped forward, needing to put a measure of distance between her and the man whose mere presence had the ability to warm her blood quicker than a double vodka martini.

She examined the expensive sculptures and artwork lining the walls, making note of the dark, creamy leather furniture and polished marble floors. Even though his summer home was grand and lavish, there was still something inviting and homey about it.

She felt him step up behind her, the warmth of his body weakening her knees as he placed his hands on her hips. "You can roam at your leisure, Rebecca," he murmured into her ear, causing the fine hairs along her neck to bristle. "The truth is, I'm not going to keep you captive."

She turned to see him, but wished she hadn't. Sexual tension arced between them, the air around them charging. She fought to recover her voice and asked, "So I *can* leave?"

"If you want to get off, you can get off." His voice dipped lower, became much deeper when he added, "But that will require you to stay."

As she caught the sexy, double entendre, her mouth opened and closed, hardly able to believe what she was hearing.

His smile turned predatory. "But you need to know that staying means following my orders."

She swallowed hard. "Look, I know what this is about. You're upset with the outcome of your trial and you brought me here for revenge."

"That's not what I'm after," he said.

"Then what exactly is it that you want from me?" She braced herself for the answer because every instinct she possessed told her revenge was exactly what he was after, and he planned to make her pay for his losses…but payment wouldn't come in the form of cash. No, it would come in another form all together.

The muscles along his jaw flexed and his black eyes shimmered when he said, "Total and utter submission."

Oh, God, the price was higher than she'd ever anticipated.

Her mouth opened, closed, and opened again, and while there were so many things she wanted to counter with, all she could do was croak out a heated moan.

"If you decide to stay, all decisions will be taken away from you." He waved a hand. "Here you don't get to ask questions or decide on anything."

Her limbs grew weak, and an unexpected lick of heat prowled through her body, settling itself deep between her legs.

"Michael will be back in a moment to collect you. You will follow him to your room, and put on only the clothes I picked out for you. Nothing more, nothing less. Then you will join me for brunch on the terrace. It's a beautiful day to eat outside, don't you think?"

Rebecca just stood there staring, her mind still processing. He wanted her to put on clothes that he picked out for her? Then meet him for brunch? Was he kidding?

Indignant, and unable to believe what he was suggesting, she drew in a quick breath to refuel her addled brain and said, "If you think I'm going to wear clothes—"

"It's not a suggestion."

As blood drained to her toes, she forced her chin up. "I thought you said you'd never make me do anything I didn't want to."

"That's correct."

"Then I don't want to wear clothes you picked out for me." She gestured to the professional pantsuit draping her body. "I have my own clothes."

He stepped closer and her heart leapt as his heat and scent overwhelmed her. "I'm a patient man, Rebecca. But we only have the weekend. And it'd be wise not to push my patience too far."

"I am not—"

"Disobedience comes with a price."

Her heart hammered. "A price?"

"I'll be forced to punish you until I have your compliance. Understand?"

"Punish…me?" she asked, a shiver moving through her, but much to her surprise it was a shiver from anticipation, not fear. She planted her hands on her hips, struggling to hold her ground. "Just how do you plan on punishing me?"

For a brief second she thought she saw the corner of his mouth curl up in a grin, but his steely control was back in place when he said, "By taking my hand to your bare ass."

"Oh, God," she squeaked out, a rush of sexual energy hitting her hard. She gulped air, and before she could get her head on straight, the vision of her draped over his lap, her ass up in the air as he spanked her, had her body quivering, almost violently.

Mr. Montgomery looked past her shoulder, and gestured with a nod. She turned to see Michael waiting for her.

"Right this way, ma'am," he said and even though she didn't want to follow him, she needed reprieve from Mr. Montgomery and the raw, sexual energy he emitted—not to mention the way it took her from a professional woman to a wanton hussy in seconds flat.

Hoping her legs didn't fail her, she made her way to her room. She took in the huge bed with its cushiony, plush bedding and pillows, then turned to see the walkout deck with its magnificent view of the ocean. On her right she spotted a private bathroom, but unfortunately her suitcase was nowhere to be found.

She turned to Michael, who pressed his hands together and said, "Please, make yourself at home. If you require anything, anything at all, press the intercom and I'll see to your needs."

"What I need are my belongings," she said.

"Mr. Montgomery will supply you with all you need during your stay." He gestured toward the bed, then disappeared into the hall, closing the door behind himself. Rebecca spun around and spotted a phone on the bedside table. So she wasn't a prisoner after all, and really could get off if she wanted to.

Her heart jumped and she hurried to it, but then another thought had her steps slowing. *Getting off would require staying...*

A low tortured moan caught in her throat and she stopped at the edge of the bed. That's when she noticed the most beautiful dress she'd ever seen splashed across her bedspread. Colored with vibrant streaks of blue and green, ocean hues that would accentuate her dark hair and blue eyes perfectly, she couldn't help but reach for it.

She touched the silky material and brought it to her face. God, it felt like butter on her skin. She shivered as she checked the tag, only to discover it was her size exactly. How? When? She held it up against her body and looked for a mirror, but then realized what she was doing. She dropped the silk back on to the bed, shook her head to get it on straight, and reached for the phone. She was not, under any circumstances, going to put on that damn dress—no matter how rich and luxurious it was —and meet that overbearing man for brunch. Nor was she going to spend one more second thinking about total and utter submission, the punishment that came with disobedience or what his large palm would feel like on her bare ass.

She didn't think…

* * *

Sunshine glistened on the Atlantic waves and a refreshing breeze washed over Quinn's body as he restlessly paced back and forth on the outside patio overlooking the ocean. Dressed for brunch in a collared shirt, and beige khaki shorts, he glanced at the beautifully set table for two, the salads and smoked salmon that Ester had prepared earlier now wilting in the late morning heat.

He shook his head. Rebecca would most definitely be punished for her tardiness. He glanced at his watch for the hundredth time, and while he knew she would come, he wondered what was taking her so long.

He'd purposely put her in a room with a phone, knowing if she wanted off this island all she'd have to do was pick up the receiver and make a call. But every instinct he possessed told him she wouldn't, and his instincts had never let him down before, in his business world or in his private one.

From the way her lush body had quivered when he spoke of spankings to the way those translucent blue eyes of her had lit with intrigue when he asked for total and utter surrender spoke volumes. She was desperate for a man to strip away the cool reserve she wore like a shield, to take all decisions out of her hands and give her what she wanted. She just didn't know what it was that she wanted yet. And soon enough she'd come to understand that this set up wasn't about kidnapping, it was about rescuing.

He pushed his hair off his head and made a move to go collect her, but when he turned she was standing in the doorway, the dress he'd had his assistant pick out earlier that morning showcasing lush curves that she foolishly kept hidden beneath severe, unflattering clothing. His cock throbbed, but unfortunately, it was too soon to take her. The submissive woman buried deep inside needed to be coaxed out slowly, carefully, because the last thing he wanted to do was frighten her off.

"What took you so long?" he asked, working to keep his cool as her gorgeous body beckoned his attention.

With her hair coiled tightly on her head, she lifted her chin, but he didn't miss the quiver in her voice when she answered with, "The only reason I'm standing here with this dress on is because I'm starving." She looked at the food on the table, and frowned.

"You shouldn't have kept me waiting." He gave her a disapproving look and continued with, "It was also unfair to Ester, who went through all this trouble for us. Now instead of taking her well-earned break, she'll have to start again." As soon as he said her name, Ester stepped outside. She gathered up the plates of spoiled food and looked to Quinn for instructions.

"Please give us a minute," he said, and she nodded in understanding before stepping back inside to give him his privacy. He turned back to Rebecca. "I'm not a man who tolerates insubordination and I don't like to waste perfectly good food."

"Neither do I. I didn't mean…I didn't think…"

"My orders were very specific. You were to dress and meet me on the terrace."

Her cheeks turned pink. "Mr. Montgomery," she began, sounding flustered as he stepped close, crowding her.

"It's Quinn."

She hesitated for a moment and he listened to her throat swallow before she began again, "Quinn, look. My intentions weren't to spoil—"

"I'm afraid you'll have to be punished for not following my orders."

She gasped, but he didn't miss the excitement backlight her big blue eyes.

Christ, she was everything he knew she would be, and he was just glad that he was the guy in charge of guiding her down the path to full sensual freedom—at least this way he'd ensure she was properly introduced and cared for in the process. A thrill moved through him, and because he hadn't felt anything so exhilarating in a long time, he grasped on to it, enjoying the sensations she aroused in him.

He stepped up to her, and she took a quick step backward, but he matched it and soon had her in his grasp. He thumbed the material of her dress, enjoying the feel of the cool silk on his fingertips before he bunched it in his palms. Pulling it higher and higher on her thighs, he slipped a hand between her legs. A cool breeze blew off the ocean and washed over them, but he suspected the quiver in her body was from his intimate touch, and not the misty air.

He looked at the bun on top of her head. "Was there an elastic on your bed?"

Her brow furrowed and her words were rushed, breathless when she asked, "No why?"

"Then why is there one in your hair?"

She blinked, looking confused for a second then answered with, "I put my hair up this morning."

"Take it out," he demanded.

He pressed his cock against her midriff, and a tremble moved through her. She lifted her arm, and then hesitated, like she was having second thoughts.

He leaned closer and spoke quieter. "I said, take it out."

Her full, lush breasts, which were high and pert in the formfitting dress, rose and fell erratically as she quickly pulled the band from her hair, letting her long dark curls fall down her back. His hands traveled higher on her thigh, only to discover that she'd once again strayed from his instructions.

In a shaky voice she began, "You weren't serious earlier, were you? I mean you're not really going to pun—"

He made a tsking sound and when he grabbed the band on her panties, giving them a good hard yank to rip them from her hips, her words were replaced with a broken gasp.

"Quinn…" she shuddered.

He tucked the scrap of material into the back pocket of his khaki shorts, and dipped back under her dress. He slid his palm along her soft, supple skin, until he reached her backside.

Testing her, he pulled her against him, and gave a slap to her ass cheek, the sound curling around them in the most sinful way. He stifled a groan, his cock throbbing and pulsating inside his unforgiving pants.

Rebecca let out a ragged cry of pleasure and Quinn kept the satisfaction from his face as he spun her around. He crushed her breasts against the exterior wall of his estate as he caged her with his chest. He put his mouth close to her neck, and whispered, "Were there panties on your bed?"

"I just thought…I decided…"

"Everything that happens here, every choice involving you is mine to make, not yours. So from this moment on, you're to stop making decisions, and enjoy the freedom that comes with that." He kept her pinned to the wall, his hard cock pressing into the small of her back. "Speaking of Freedom, that is your safe word."

"Freedom?" she murmured, her voice husky.

"Yes, if you don't like what is happening, all you have to do is say that one word and I'll stop."

She angled her head to see him and when she opened her mouth, like she was about to speak the word that would put an end to her initiation into the BDSM world before he even began, he warned, "Be careful, Rebecca. Only use it when you really mean it, only when something is happening that you don't want. But you can be assured that I plan to give you everything you want."

A noise caught in her throat and he sensed her mounting desire when she shifted her hips, pushing up against him. The movement was slight, but it was a clear sign that she wanted this to happen every bit as much as he did.

He cupped her ass, sliding the silk material over her lush contours, and she hissed in response to his soft seduction, which was about to turn a little rough and forceful, the way she needed it.

"Now, about this punishment…"

When her knees seemed to give, he anchored her to his body and walked her to the table. He sank down into one of the chairs and her dark lashes blinked rapidly over expressive blue eyes, her hair falling seductively over her shoulders as she stood there staring at him. Quinn couldn't help but smile at her compliance, at how fast she was catching on. It takes a very strong woman to submit, and an even stronger one to do it so quickly.

He lifted her dress to expose her sex, his smile widening. "Such a pretty pussy." He reached out and stroked her satiny lips, a growl rising in his throat. "Shaved so nicely. Just the way I like it." His glance met hers. "It's almost like you knew."

As delight danced in her eyes at his praise, he gripped her hips, laid her across his lap, and took full control of her body as he prepared to divvy out equal amounts of pain and pleasure. He lifted her dress to expose her perfect backside, and oddly enough passion and possession moved through his blood, because there was something very profound, very moving in knowing that Rebecca was trusting him so honestly and openly, gifting him with her body in a way she'd never given it to another.

He drew in air to center himself, because there was no denying that he'd dreamt about this moment for a long time, no denying that there was something about this woman that had the ability to breathe new life into him.

It was all he could do to keep his hands from shaking when he caressed her lightly, then lifted his hand to give her creamy skin a good hard whack.

She squealed, and he pressed a hand to her back to still her.

"Oh. My. God," she cried out.

He smacked her again, the bright red outline of his palm on her ass filling him with a new kind of hunger. He widened her legs, and when the sweet scent of her arousal reached his nostrils, he clenched down hard. He slipped his hand between her creamy thighs and she move against him, her actions so telling. She needed release. She needed him.

"Next time," he said, coming perilously close to her clit, but never touching. "I expect you to do exactly as instructed."

"Yes," she cried out, grinding her pussy on his thigh.

He widened her pretty pink lips, and he could feel the impatience thrumming inside her. Her clit was so swollen and ready, and with just the right about of pressure he knew he could get her off. But disobedience was never rewarded, and that would be her first lesson.

She writhed, but he pulled his hand away from her cunt. "Bad girls are punished, not rewarded."

"Quinn…"

"Yes?" he asked, sliding his hand to her ass to give her another hard slap.

A cry lodged in her throat as the sound carried in the breeze. "I need you to touch me. I'm so close. Put your fingers inside me. Now," she demanded.

He exhaled slowly. "You don't get to make decisions or demands, Rebecca. Have you already forgotten that I'm in charge of you and I'll decide when you come?"

Hot and wet, her liquid heat glistened in the sun as her pretty pink pussy cried out for his attention. As much as he wanted to put a finger inside her, to stroke deep and bring her to orgasm, it wasn't part of his training. He removed his hands from her body, leaving her aching for more.

Ignoring her cries of protest, he lifted her from his lap. With her hair in disarray, and her dress gathered around her hips, she stood before him, her chest heaving, her mouth opening and closing in gasping fits. She flicked him a glance, her expression a mixture of embarrassment and frustration as she stood there, like she was waiting further instructions.

Good girl.

He studied her for a long time, then said, "Fix yourself."

She obliged and when Ester came out with their food, Quinn stood and pulled a chair out for Rebecca. He leaned into her and whispered, "Please sit and enjoy this lovely food that Ester has once again prepared for us."

Looking mortified, Rebecca glanced at the food, then averted her gaze. "I…I have to go."

"Sit down, Rebecca."

She visibly shivered as she lowered herself in to her chair, and when Quinn put his mouth close to her ear, and whispered, "You did good, Rebecca," his words of praise seemed to do something to her, give her a sense of purpose.

"When you learn to obey, you'll be rewarded. But in the meantime, don't even think about touching yourself to finish what I started. If you do, I'll know, and punishment will be twice as severe."

Three

Rebecca paced inside her room, having endured one of the most confusing, yet exciting mornings of her life. She sat on her bed, only to rise again, the sting on her ass cheeks a blissful reminder of her punishment.

Her punishment…

Oh God how could she have liked it so much? How could she have submitted to him, putting herself at his mercy and allowing him to do whatever he pleased to her?

She shook her head hard and wrung her hands together, and as she thought about the way he dominated her a barrage of emotions coursed through her veins.

She didn't want this.

She couldn't.

Intelligent, successful, driven women like her didn't hand themselves over to a man. No, they took control, set the pace and parameters in a relationship and made all the decisions, inside the bedroom and out. Right? They surely didn't tolerate spankings or readily submit upon command.

But you know you want to.

Confused and still quivering all over, she walked to the window to look out. When she spotted Quinn near the shore, standing at the wharf looking pensive with his legs wide and his arms behind his back, her breath caught. Wondering if he still had her panties in his pocket, she stared at him for a long moment, her pussy quivering, in desperate need of attention after their sexually charged brunch together.

Widening her legs slightly, she slipped a hand between her thighs, touching herself through the silk material. Her pussy quivered, and her clit swelled beneath her touch, but then she quickly pulled her hand away, wanting to please him and obey his every command.

Oh God, she really did want this…

A knock sounded on her door, and she spun around. She pulled it open to find Michael standing there, a package in his hand. "Mr. Montgomery would like you to wear this to dinner tonight. You will dine on the beach, eight sharp. I will come collect you ten minutes early. Until then, please explore and enjoy the island."

The second he left she hurried to her bed, far more excited than she should be to see what he wanted her to wear. She pulled open the package and inside found an exquisite cocktail dress, and pair of high heels, along with a black bustier and matching thong. She fingered the sexy outfit, one she never would have had the nerve to buy for herself, but had to admit, couldn't wait to try on. As a jolt of excitement moved through her, she worked to tamp it down, but she was well past the point of denying that she wanted to submit to Quinn…wanted him to take full control.

Her fingers shook as she neatly folded the clothes and put them back on her bed. She checked the clock, and wondered how she would ever make it to eight. Needing to occupy her mind to pass the time, and keep her thoughts busy with something other than what might happen tonight, she slipped from her room and made her way to the water. She explored the grounds and exchanged greetings with a man, who she could only assume was Mario, as he tended to the foliage. Her glance kept straying to the wharf to where she'd spotted Quinn earlier. Disappointment settled in her gut when he was nowhere to be found.

The rest of the day passed slowly, much too slowly for her liking. The drawn out afternoon merely served as tortuous foreplay, sexual tension growing in her body with each passing second. She forced herself to explore the island, waving to those cruising by on their sailboats. With surrounding islands, occupied by vacationers, Quinn's estate wasn't as isolated as she had first thought, and if she really wanted to, she easily could have flagged down help and gotten herself off this island.

But you don't want to…

That thought had her rushing back to her room. She took a quick glance at the clock, and jumped in the shower to get ready. After cleansing her body with some delectable strawberry scented shampoo and soap, she towel dried, and out of habit gathered her hair in a ponytail to tie it back, but a fine shiver moved through her when she remember he hadn't left her an elastic band.

She let her hair dry naturally, her curls more pronounced as they cascaded down her back. Naked, she stepped into the bedroom and her heart picked up tempo as she slowly began to dress in the clothes he'd laid out for her. As she put each piece on, she wondered if Quinn would removed them, and if so how. Slowly? Furiously? Pressure brewed deep between her legs, and her clit throbbed…*throbbed* for his attention.

Once she was dressed, feeling desirable and sexy in the frilly underthings that fit her body to perfection, she gave herself a once-over in the mirror. She had never felt so feminine in her entire life. When the knock came at ten minutes to eight, she drew a breath to steady herself and slipped into her sexy shoes.

Michael smiled as he looked her over. "Mr. Montgomery will be pleased," he said, and as soon as the words left his mouth, she realized how happy that made her, how much she wanted to please him, wanted his praise. With a wave to set her in motion, he led the way to the beach, to a gorgeous, candlelit table in the sand, the ocean providing a breathtaking, romantic backdrop.

She was about to take her seat at the empty table, when a hand on the small of her back stopped her. "I see today's punishment has taught you a lesson about tardiness."

"Yes," she murmured breathlessly, although for a brief moment she had considered coming late, knowing full well what the punishment would entail. Quinn pulled her chair out for her and she sat. He then moved to the other side of the table, and when she caught his glance, her heart leapt. With heat and hunger on his face, his eyes moved over her.

"You look beautiful."

"Thank you. But how did you know my size?" She looked at the expensive designer cocktail dress. "Where did you get all these clothes?"

Instead of answering, he just smiled, poured her a glass of wine and handed it to her. "Are you hungry?"

As soon as she nodded, Ester came with salads. Rebecca took a sip of wine in an effort to settle her anxiety, then picked up her fork, but the nervousness, the excitement in her stomach made it almost impossible to eat.

"Did you enjoy your day?" Quinn began, and she sensed he was making small talk in a bid to relax her.

"Yes, it's beautiful here. The view is breathtaking and the sea air is rejuvenating."

He arched a knowing brow. "I thought you could use some time to yourself after brunch, which is why I left you alone for such an extended period."

He was right, she did need time to examine what had happened between them, and come to terms with how this weekend would play out, how much she *wanted* it to play out.

"But do know that for the rest of your time here, you won't be left alone. You will be under my care at all times."

Under his care…

Her throat tightened and she couldn't believe how much she liked the sound of that. She picked at her food, too excited to eat as she thought about putting herself in his hands again. Quinn seemed to notice her anxiety, which she couldn't seem to hide.

He wiped his mouth with his cloth napkin, then set it beside his plate. "Have you lost your appetite, Rebecca?" he asked, genuine concern in his eyes.

She looked at him, and said, "Maybe a little."

He pulled his chair out from the table. "Come here."

Oh God.

He cocked his head, his eyes assessing her. "What has you so nervous?"

"This…you," she admitted quietly, lowering her eyes.

"Does this make you so uncomfortable that you want to use your safe word?"

She exhaled slowly. "No."

"Have you been thinking about your punishment earlier today?"

"Yes."

"Is your pussy still hot and wet, like it was when I put my hand to your bare ass?'

"Yes," she croaked out.

"Look at me, Rebecca."

When she met his dark gaze he asked, "You didn't touch yourself did you?"

"No. You told me not to so I didn't."

That brought smile to his face and her insides leapt with pleasure. "That's a good girl, Rebecca. And like I told you earlier, good girls get rewarded."

God, yes…

He sat back in his chair and silence hung for a long time. Her inside twisted with desire as she waited to see what came next, not daring to make the next move, and loving that the decision wasn't hers to make. That realization shocked her, but more importantly, excited her beyond anything she'd ever known. Honestly, she had no idea how much she wanted this until he'd spanked her, until he asked her to submit to him. She wasn't sure how, but the powerful Quinn Montgomery had somehow tapped into her deepest, darkest desire—ones she didn't even know she had until now—and forced her to examine herself from the inside out.

And she was damn grateful he had…

"I assume you wore the lingerie I left for you."

She nodded.

"Don't nod at me. Speak."

"Yes," she answered. "I wore the lingerie."

"Show me."

Moisture broke out on her skin and she glanced around, aware that his staff was milling about, and here, near the ocean, with candles outlining their silhouette, if someone happened to sail by, they'd be able to see her.

"Show me," he repeated, only harsher, the warning clear in his tone.

A small noise sounded in her throat as she released the zipper at the back of her dress, allowing it to slip from her body and puddle at her feet. Quinn just sat there, taking his time to look at her body in the sexy clothes he'd obviously chosen with care.

"You have a beautiful body. You shouldn't keep it covered." A long pause then, "Come closer."

She stepped toward him, her shoes sinking in the sand.

"Take off your shoes."

She slipped out of the heels, the sand warm beneath her toes.

"Get on your knees."

She sank to her knees before him, and he cupped her chin. He lifted her face until her eyes met his. Then his hand trailed over her cheek, her neck, until he reached her cleavage. He lightly touched her, feathering his thumb over her breasts, before trailing his fingers back to her mouth. He brushed the pad of his thumb over her bottom lip, then pushed it inside her mouth.

"Show me how you suck," he said.

Rebecca closed her mouth around his thumb and sucked deeply, using her tongue to brush the rough tip. When she heard a tortured moan, her body quaked, hoping...*praying*, he'd replace his thumb with his cock. Her mouth watered for him, aching to be stretched and filled, pushed beyond her limits.

He pulled his thumb out and ran it along her neck, wetting her skin with her saliva. "Do you like to suck cock, Rebecca?"

She nodded, but then remembered she was supposed to speak. "Yes."

His voice dropped an octave. "Would you like to suck mine?"

"I would."

As Quinn stood, and unbuckled his pants, she shivered in anticipation. With his instructions clear, she released his cock, and when she caught a glimpse of his impressive size and girth, her womb clenched with need. To know she could make him this hard, to visually see how much he wanted her, brought her to a whole new level of excitement. He fisted her hair as she leaned toward him, determined to please him.

She gripped his cock, and he jutted his hips forward, feeding it into her waiting mouth. She widened her lips, taking in as much as she possibly could, but when he said, "No hands," she let them fall to her sides.

She rocked back and forth, spending a long time pleasuring him. Her moans grew louder when she tasted the salty cream dripping from the tip, and she wondered if he'd release in her mouth, shoot his hot seed down her throat. He growled and his muscles bunched as his veins filled with blood, but before he gave himself over, he gripped her shoulders and pulled her off.

"Stand up," he demanded as he tucked his cock away and zipped up his pants.

She climbed to her feet and he sat back in his chair as she stood before him, waiting for his instructions.

"Show me your breasts."

Ripples of pleasure moved through her as she removed her bustier, the misty ocean breeze pebbling her already hard nipples.

Quinn pushed her hair off her shoulder, put his finger into her mouth, brushing it over her tongue to wet it, then scraped it over her pebbled nubs. She bit back a breathy moan and leaned into his touch.

"Don't do that," he said, his voice rough. "Just stand still while I touch you, and don't make a sound until I tell you to." She sucked in a breath and he trailed his hand over her breasts, stroking them gently before pinching her nipple, hard.

She wanted to cry out but she'd been given a direct order, so instead she remained quiet, waiting to see what came next. He pinched harder, to the point of blissful pain, and then he rose from his chair. With slow, unhurried movements he circled her, and when he moved behind her, her ass bare to him in her thong, he lightly trailed his hands over her tender backside, and put his mouth near her ear.

"It's almost a shame you weren't tardy tonight," he whispered, his hot breath doing delicious things to her senses. "Your ass looks like it could use another spanking."

He dropped to his knees and she swallowed, the sound carrying in the night as he paid homage to her round cheeks, touching gently and kissing away the sting that his hand had left behind earlier. She wanted to move, wiggle, push up against him, but found excitement in following his rules and remaining quiet and motionless.

He gripped the elastic on her thong and gave a little tug downward. "Now let me see that pretty cunt of yours. Let me see if it's hot and wet for me."

He stood, moved back in front of her and reclaimed his chair. "Take your panties off," he ordered.

She gripped the scrap of lace, and slid them down her legs. She lifted one foot then the other, until she was stark naked and shaking from want.

"Now hand them to me."

His deep voice made her toes curl as she passed them over and he brought them to his nose to inhale her scent before tucking them in his pocket. Holding her gaze, he called out for Ester, and when Rebecca made a move to cover herself, aware that his cook would see her naked, he gave a slow shake of his head to stop her, the cold warning in his eyes stilling her hands.

Ester stepped from the shadows. "Please clear the table, Ester. Then you may take the rest of the night off to do as you please."

"Your food, sir?" she asked.

"Chill it for later. There is only one thing I'm interested in feasting on right now."

"Very well," she said as Rebecca's knees quivered in anticipation. With her breasts heavy and her pussy on display, she watched Ester removed the dishes and carry them back to the estate at the top of the hill.

Quinn adjusted his chair, positioning it at the table like he was preparing to eat a meal. "Lay yourself out for me." He waved his hand over the wood. "Right here."

Blood pumping madly, she shimmied on to the table and laid back, her pussy merely inches from his face as her legs dangled over the edge.

"Widen your legs and show me your cunt."

She did as he commanded, and as she stared at the mosaic of stars in the night sky, she waited impatiently, waited for that first sweet touch of his tongue.

A finger moved over her slit. "Have you been this hot and wet for me all day?"

"Yes," she answered.

She could feel his breath on her inner thighs, so hot and moist it was all she could do not to cry out. "You were a very good girl not to touch yourself. Your sweet cunt is mine to play with not yours. Understand?"

Desperate for him to play with it now, to lick, suck and fuck her, she murmured, "Yes." Cream dripped down her leg, and she was sure if he didn't soon touch her, she would go up in a burst of flame. She listened for him to speak, to do something, but silence hovered for a long time.

Seconds passed.

Minutes.

She waited for what felt like a lifetime.

And then it happened.

Like fire on her skin, his tongue swiped from the bottom to the top, and as heat bombarded her, she felt a soft quake in the center of her core. Glorious. So damn glorious. He licked her again, and she spasmed. God, she was close, already so damn close she wasn't sure how much more she could take.

He flicked the soft blade of his tongue over her clit and moaned in pleasure. "I've never tasted anything so sweet," he said from deep between her legs. Passion raced through her and she shivered under his invasive touch.

He inserted a finger and just kept it there, not moving, not stroking, simply filling her with its girth. It was blissful torture designed to let her know he was in charge. Fueled by need she writhed and moaned in sheer frustration.

"Keep still, Rebecca and you are not to come until I tell you to."

He put another finger inside her, and the fit was so snug, so deliciously tight all she wanted to do was move, force him to pump deep and bring her to climax.

"Such a lovely tight cunt," he said, as he drew her clit into his mouth. "My cock is going to fill you so nicely."

Yes...

He slowly, methodically began to move his fingers inside her, pressing, pushing, and building a powerful climax. How would she ever hang on? But she had to. He'd told her to.

She drew a shaky breath and stole a glance at the amazing man feasting on her. Honestly, until this moment, this man, she had no idea why her past relationships had all failed. But now she knew. She didn't want an easy considerate lover, a man who let her control the play, take the reins. No. She wanted this. Domination. Total and utter surrender.

Oh God, she wanted this…

His fingers stopped moving and he climbed to his feet. His dark, hungry glance met hers. "Fuck my fingers. Move your hips and fuck my fingers like a good girl."

Rebecca gripped the sides of the table and started moving, meeting each thrust as he pumped into her and stroked her clit. She closed her eyes and concentrated on the points of pleasure, but then she opened them again, and tossed her head from side to side. Desperate to come, to give in to the sensations, her breath came in ragged bursts.

"What is it, Rebecca?"

"I'm going to come."

"Not until I say so. You can hang on."

"Quinn…please…"

"Don't disobey me, Rebecca," he warned.

He stroked harder, applied more pressure, and her body began tingling, every nerve quivering and on fire. She breathed against the blinding pressure, letting it build higher and higher until she hovered on the precipice. Heat whipped through her and her thoughts fragmented. He leaned over her and drew a nipple in his mouth, the wet heat of his tongue magnificent on her flesh. He sucked hard, and she stifled a cry when he bit down. As she hovered on the brink of orgasm, barely a shred of sanity left, his gaze met hers.

"Come for me," he whispered, and just like that she gave herself over to the pleasure. She cried out in relief, her pussy convulsing and clenching tightly around his fingers, holding them deep inside her body as her voice rose higher and higher. Waves of ecstasy lashed her body with the same ferocity as the waves crashing against the jagged rocks below. She gasped for breath, never having felt anything so powerful or amazing in her entire life. He held her as she trembled, wrapping her in his arms, and the possession she caught in his eyes when they moved over her face filled her with a new kind of need.

When her body stopped spasming, Quinn unzipped his pants, gripped her hips to pull her to the edge of the table, and without speaking, drove his cock all the way inside her. His nostrils flared and his fingers dug into her soft flesh as he pounded into her, fucking her like a man hell-bent on taking what was his. As he ravaged her, her heart raced, loving that he wanted her like this, with such passion and possession. He fucked harder and faster, like he couldn't get deep enough, like he was seeking more than just release. It excited her, frightened her, made her feel wanted and cherished.

"You're mine, Rebecca," he growled.

"Quinn…" she murmured.

"Say it."

"I'm yours."

"This is my cunt, and I'm the only one who gets to fuck it."

"Yes," she cried out as his words, and his savage fucking, brought her to the edge again. His fingers bit deeper into her flesh and she knew he'd leave a bruise. But she wanted to be marked by him, a token to remember this moment. He shifted for deeper penetration, and she arched into him. Her entire body broke out in a sweat, and she moaned as a second climax swept through her.

"Jesus," he cried out, as she let go, her hot cream coating his cock. A second later he threw his head back and came on a growl. He depleted himself high inside her, and she tightened, milking him of every last drop.

He fell over her, his heart pounding against her body. He stayed like that until his breathing settled, then he pulled his cock out, and re-zipped his pants. Rebecca remained still, sprawled out on the table, her mind still not functioning properly.

Quinn gripped her hands and pulled her until she was sitting upright.

Feeling completely comfortable in her skin around him, and basking in the new intimacy they now shared, she glanced at her clothes in the sand, waiting for him to instruct her to dress.

He ran his hand down her arm, the touch achingly gentle, and the tenderness on his face when his eyes met hers made her breath catch. "You have a beautiful body and I have decided that for the duration of your stay here, I want you naked."

Rebecca gulped air. "What about your staff?"

"What about them?"

"I can't walk around naked in front of them."

"You can and you will."

"But Quinn…"

"And I meant what I said, Rebecca. Your cunt is mine. Mine to do with as I please."

Four

Quinn put his arm around Rebecca's slim waist and guided her back to the estate. Once inside, he led her to his suite—specifically to his impressive private bathroom. He turned on one of the many spray nozzles inside the large, walk-in shower and looked at the incredible woman who'd made him feel things he hadn't felt in years.

When he smiled at her, she asked, "What?"

"Still want to run away?"

She returned his smile. "No." Then she bit her lip and said, "You knew I wouldn't make the call didn't you?"

Quinn stepped into the shower and held his hand out for her. "Yes, now come here and let me wash you." He adjusted the spray and put her under it. She moaned in ecstasy and he grabbed the soap to lather her. He washed her body, taking extra care with her bruised pussy before teasing the tight rosette between her ass cheeks, gauging her reaction which was hesitant but positive. He pressed a finger in to test her and when her eyes widened, his heart leapt, thrilled to know he would be the first guy to penetrate her anally. His cock twitched in anticipation, but he banked his desires, knowing they'd have plenty of time for that later. He gathered her hair, and poured a generous amount of shampoo into his hands before he began to wash her long curls.

She whimpered in delight. "I love the way you take care of me."

"You've given yourself to me, Rebecca and it's my responsibility to take care of you." When she blinked up at him, he explained. "I take that responsibility very seriously."

Her brow furrowed. "You'll always take care of me?"

"Yes. It's part of the Dom/sub relationship. I will tell you what you can and cannot do, but I always have your best interests at heart. You do understand that don't you?"

She nodded, and he pulled her close, running his soapy hands over her body to finish cleaning her. He slipped a hand back between her legs. "Is your pussy sore?"

"A little."

"If I'm ever too rough, you know you have a safe word, right?"

She shook her head. "I love how you took what you needed."

He held her tight, his heart pounding with the understanding that he'd never felt so close to anyone before. "But I'll never take without giving. Not with you, Rebecca."

"I love that, too." She went quiet for a moment, then asked, "How did you know, when I didn't even know?"

"It was the way you shied away from me during proceeding. The sub in you sensed the Dom in me. I knew what you needed long before you did, and I wanted to be the man to give it to you, which is why I brought you here, and not to Freedom."

"Oh," she said. "You remember me from way back then."

"I've never forgotten you, Rebecca."

"I've never forgotten you either," she admitted, then her eyes widened like she was remembering something else. "Wait, we didn't use protection."

"You're on the pill."

"How did you know?"

He smiled. "Because I took great pain in learning everything about you before I brought you here." He touched her chin, and angled her face upward. "And don't worry. I'm clean. I'm tested monthly."

Her stomach took that moment to grumble and Quinn laughed. "Come on. Let's get dried off and have some dinner and wine on the bedroom patio."

Quinn wrapped her in a big fluffy towel, knowing the night breeze would be cool up here on the hill. He led her outside, and she took a seat, contentment written all over her.

She glanced at the ocean, her eyes wide and full of new life.

"So beautiful."

His heart missed a beat and he said truthfully, "There is no one else I'd rather be sharing this with."

She looked at the towel and her eyes widened. She made a move to shed it. "Oh…"

He stopped her. "No. Tonight you will stay wrapped. It's chilly, and I wouldn't want you to be uncomfortable. In the heat of the day, you will be remain uncovered, but for now, keep this on."

Something moved over her face, and his heart pinched.

"I love the way you take care of me," she said quietly.

"Good, because I don't ever plan to stop."

She exhaled slowly, and he dropped a kiss onto her mouth. "I'll go round us up some food and drink. Then once those needs are taken care of, I do plan to take you again."

He turned and made a quick trip to the kitchen to reheat the food Ester had prepared for them earlier, then grabbed a bottle of wine.

When he went back to his bedroom and saw Rebecca sitting on his patio, like it was where she always belonged, he knew in an instant that he could never be with another. She was his sub, he was her Dom and he would spend his life taking care of her, and pleasing her.

* * *

Rebecca woke to the sound of waves splashing in the distance. She stretched out her sore limbs and smiled because it was a good sore. One that reminded her of all the deliciously naughty things she did with Quinn since arriving on this majestic island.

God, how could she have gotten so lucky, to be kidnapped and awakened sexually by this magnificent man who took such care in introducing her to the darker side of pleasure. She might not have made it to Freedom, but never had she felt so free.

"Good morning."

She looked at Quinn, and was about to speak when he pulled her to him. He kissed her long and hard, then climbed over her, pinning her beneath him. Their tongues tangled as she widened her legs for him, granting him access to her body and heart.

When his cock found home, he pumped into her, their lovemaking hot and passionate and every bit as moving as it was the last time. Rebecca basked in the sensation, never wanting the feeling, or this wild weekend, to end. After lovemaking, they showered and Quinn took her to the beach where they nibbled on fresh fruit and delicious omelettes made by Ester, who was now arranging towels and what looked like a picnic basket on the sand, close to the surf. As Rebecca sat across from him, stark naked, a warm breeze on her flesh, they talked quietly, but she didn't miss the hunger in his eyes.

Before she realized it, she was in Quinn's arms again. "I can't seem to get enough of you."

"You should probably do something about that."

His eyes darkened as he led her to the towels that Ester had arranged for him. Once there he spun Rebecca around, his hands going to her breasts as he pushed up against her. She could feel his hard cock press against the small of her back, and feeling naughty, wanting a spanking, she wiggled up against him.

He slid his hand along her hips, then cupped her ass cheek. "If you're going to tease me with your sweet ass, then I'll have no choice but to take it."

She gasped, remembering how he inserted a finger during their shower. Was he really planning on fucking her anally?

"Quinn…" she murmured nervously.

"Remember what I said, Rebecca. I will always take care of you."

Her heart raced as he dropped to his knees behind her, and when she felt his warm lips on her cheek, her body quaked.

"Such a pretty, pretty ass," he murmured, desire making his voice husky.

Oh God…

He slid a hand to her pussy, dipped into her liquid heat, the trailed it over her back opening. She remained still, curious and frightened as he teased a finger inside. It felt strange, uncomfortable, but the truth was she wanted this, wanted him to take her in a way no man had ever taken her before.

"Widen your legs." She did as he requested, and stood there bared to him looking out over the water as he prepared her ass, pushing one, then two fingers past her ringed passage. When she tightened he rubbed her clit, and said, "Relax for me. Let me take care of you."

She exhaled slowly and let him stretch her. He stood back up, and slid his hand around her waist. He put his mouth near her ear and said, "Get down on your hands and knees."

Breathing labored, she dropped to the towel, wondering how she'd ever accommodate his huge cock, but trusting in Quinn enough to know he'd never hurt her.

"Look at you," he murmured. "Your ass is just craving to be fucked."

She listened to the hiss of his zipper, then he dropped down behind her. He opened the basket and pulled out a tube of lube. He squirted it into his hand, and then coated her puckered rosette.

The liquid felt cool at first, but then began warming. He worked his fingers back into her ass, and his growl of longing curled around her. Her nipples tightened, and when she relaxed into his touch she could feel her body opening.

"That's it, Rebecca. That's it exactly."

A quake moved through her, her body responding to the pleasure in his voice.

He removed his fingers and she could feel his crown breach her opening. He moved slowly, offering her only an inch at a time and allowing her to get used to the feeling before going deeper. Pain and pleasure hit at the same time, and when he drove deeper, stretching her unnaturally, her body clenched.

"Easy," he said, running his hands along her back, his soft whisper covering her like a blanket.

She breathed slowly, wanting this, wanting to make this good for him. Quinn reached around and rubbed her clit, as he pushed deeper. Feeling like he was ripping her, she gasped, and even though she knew she could put a stop to this, use her safe word if she wanted to, she clamped her mouth shut and let him take full possession of her.

She relaxed again, her muscles loosening. "That's a girl." He stroked her back gently. "You're doing so good, Rebecca. I wish you could see the way my cock is sliding into your ass. You are so sexy, so beautiful like this." He jerked his hips and they both groaned. "Look at that, I'm almost all the way inside you now."

His words, and the pleasure she heard behind them, was all the encouragement she needed. She pushed back against him, taking him the rest of the way into her body.

"Fuck," he bit out.

Rebecca began panting and he stayed still inside her for a long time. Sunlight spilled over their bodies, until hunger consumed her. She needed him to fuck her, to come inside her and claim her like this.

She moved her body to let him know she was ready. Quinn gripped her hips, and began moving. Slowly at first, then quicker, lust getting the better of him. He bent over her and rubbed her clit, taking her on the journey to ecstasy right along with him. Everything in what they were doing was highly erotic, deeply intimate, bringing them closer and closer together.

Pressure began brewing in her body, her orgasm approaching rapidly.

"You are mine and mine alone," Quinn said.

"Yes, Quinn," she said, tension growing in her body. "I am yours to take."

"Now come for me."

She gripped the beach towel beneath her, squeezing the cotton as she climaxed. Her cries carried in the breeze and when Quinn let go, releasing himself in her ass, emotions brought tears to her eyes.

He collapsed onto her back, and wrapped his hands around her waist to hold her tight. He remained inside her until his cock grew flaccid, then he pulled out. He dropped beside her and pulled her down, holding her head against his chest. She stayed there, listening to the pounding of his heart, and knew there was no place she'd rather be, no man she'd rather be with.

You are mine and mine alone.

As she thought about what he said, she wondered if he meant it, or was that just something a Dom said as his passion peaked.

Quinn climbed to his feet and pulled her up with him. "How about a swim?" When she caught the tenderness in his eyes, it had her wondering if it was it possible that he'd want to continue with this relationship when they returned home. Then again, what if this weekend was it, and when they returned home they'd both go back to their lives?

Her stomach tightened because she had no idea how she could go back to dating nice, kind men, who had no idea what she wanted in a relationship. She pushed that disheartening thought aside and decided now was not the time to dwell on it. Now was the time to enjoy Quinn, and this island, and forget about reality for awhile.

"I'd love to," she said, hoping her voice didn't sound as shaky as her insides.

The rest of the day and night was spent in each other's arms, and they woke to a glorious Sunday where they played in the surf and made love beneath the sun. Before she realized it, Sunday night was upon them, and it was time to head back to reality.

After their last lovemaking session a little over an hour ago, Quinn had instructed her to go to her room to pack. Dressed in a pantsuit not at all unlike the one she'd arrived in, and leaving the clothes behind that Quinn had purchased for her, her heart felt heavy as she sealed her suitcase. She swallowed the knot in her throat, her gut warning that this could very well be the last she was going to see of Quinn, considering he hadn't made mention of seeing her or continuing with their relationship when they left this idyllic island behind.

A knock came on her door and she hurried to it, but disappointment settled in her stomach when she found Michael there to collect her.

"Mr. Montgomery is ready to escort you back home."

She followed him to the plane, and took her seat in the back as Quinn, who was once again dressed in his flight suit, flew her back home. She sat quietly, and while she tried to catch his attention, he kept his eyes forward and his focus on the controls. A long time later they landed, and she tried not to appear as apprehensive as she felt when he opened her door to help her from the plane. His crew came to greet him and tend to the plane. He spoke to them as she stood there waiting for instructions, waiting to see what came next but her heart fell into her stomach when he asked, "Do you have a ride?"

"I left my car in underground parking."

"Very well." He gave a curt nod. "Have a safe drive home, Ms. Andrews."

Swallowing against the tightness in her throat, and hating that things were ending this way, she made her way to her car. Blurry eyed, she drove the short trip home, and once inside her condo, she collapsed on her bed, exhaustion and heartache pulling at her as she fell into a fitful sleep.

Before she realized it, her alarm went off, and after hitting the snooze button, she climbed from her bed in need of coffee. As she walked to her closet to pull on her robe, she wondered what she'd wear to work, suddenly hating her entire wardrobe, hating that she had to make the choice each and every morning. Moving numbly and trying not to think of Quinn, she walked to the kitchen in desperate need of coffee, but the knock on her door startled her.

She hurried to it, hoping to find Quinn on the other side, but terrified that she wouldn't. She pulled it open and found a courier standing there, a beautifully wrapped gift box in his hand.

"Please sign here," he said, looking rather bored.

Pulse leaping, she scribbled her name down, and rushed to her kitchen table, shaking the light box as she went. She tore off paper, then removed the lid, setting aside the note as the beautiful dress inside gained her full attention.

Quinn…

She pulled the silk from the box and held it to her, the material so soft and luxurious against her body. The dress was professional enough for work—which touched her deeply, because it showed how much he truly cared for her and the image she needed to maintain as a lawyer—yet it was still sexy and sophisticated and would showcase her curves in a classy, stylish way.

She searched the box, pulling out the tissue paper until she came upon a push-up bra, but no panties to be found. A moan of excitement bubbled in her throat and her pussy quivered in erotic delight as she thought about going to work sans panties, with no one it the world knowing but her and Quinn.

As she thought about all the things he did to her, for her, during their whirlwind weekend, she ripped open the note. As she read it, her heart leapt with joy, knowing she was the luckiest woman in the world to have such an attentive and wonderful Dom like Quinn caring for her.

Emotions rose in her and heat settled deep between her legs but there was nothing she could do to contain her squeal of delight rising from her throat when she read the note a second time.

"You are to wear this to work, and nothing else. I will be by to see you at some point during the day, and if I discover that you've strayed from my instructions...*you will be punished.*"

Yours to Teach

One

Perched on the edge of her plush office chair, Rebecca Andrews stared at the open files strewn across her desktop. She blinked, and then widened her eyes in an attempt to concentrate, but all she could see was a blur of white paper and black ink, the words nothing but a foggy haze. Pinching the bridge of her nose, she pulled in a breath and blew it out slowly. She had to focus, get her thoughts on track and on her job.

Annoyed with her lack of self-control, Rebecca shook her head and gathered the papers. She shuffled them into a neat little pile, hoping that would somehow help her concentration. But how could she possibly think about planning a defense for an upcoming trial when visions of the powerful and enigmatic Quinn Montgomery were at the forefront of her mind?

She sank back into the buttery brown leather and stared at the white ceiling tiles. As she settled into the cushiony warmth, her thoughts strayed to last Saturday morning and the unexpected turn of events that had opened her eyes to her long-suppressed sexual needs.

After her last in a long line of breakups, her friends had gifted her with a ticket to a sex resort called Freedom, feeling she needed to loosen up, kick back and stop trying to control everyone and everything in her life. Her plans, however, had veered off course, literally, and she never made it to the resort. Instead, Quinn Montgomery, pilot and owner of an entire fleet of airplanes, had pseudo-kidnapped her and flown her to his oceanfront summer villa on his private island off the coast of Nova Scotia where he'd shown her that submitting her body to him held the most powerful control of all. Who knew that deep down she was a submissive at heart, one who craved to be taken over her Dom's knee and spanked until her backside turned pink? If it weren't for Quinn, and his commanding yet caring touch, she never would have known the pleasure of submitting her body to another, would never have known what had been missing from her life or why she'd been so bored with the guys she'd dated in the past.

Her pulse kicked up a notch and she sat up straighter, letting out a fluttery breath as she recalled the scandalous things he'd done to her body. Her hands, as though operating independently from her brain, moved to her legs, where her skin still burned from his touch. Her fingers curled in the silk material of her skirt, pulling the fabric up her thighs to expose her bare legs and a hint of her black panties beneath—panties that Quinn would punish her for wearing.

Quinn...

Her thoughts hurried back to the Monday morning after her incredible weekend with him, and the surprise she'd found waiting for her. After two glorious days of mind-blowing sex, she'd awakened back in her Manhattan condo to a present from Quinn—

a beautiful dress and a note that instructed her to wear it to work and nothing else. She did as requested, and had spent the entire day a jittery mess of anticipation, only to receive a text from him to let her know he had out-of-town business to attend to. Now here it was late Friday afternoon, and he'd yet to text her again, show up at her office, or make any further contact with her.

As the owner of Montgomery Charters, and one of the world's youngest self-made billionaires, she knew he was a busy man with many responsibilities, but his charter made daily runs to Freedom, and for all she knew he'd flown there himself and spent the week playing—without her. Which made her wonder if he'd had a change of heart and things were over between them. Perhaps the weekend at his summer villa actually had been his way of getting revenge, awakening her submissive side, setting it free only to walk away and leave her wanting more—the cruelest form of payback for taking him down in the courtroom a little over a year ago.

She sprang from her chair, her skirt falling over her knees as she walked to the window and slid it open. She listened the rush of traffic on the busy Manhattan streets below and wished she'd never met Quinn. Her hands shook as she smoothed them down her hips. Arrogant bastard. If she'd never known the pleasure of his touch she wouldn't have known what she'd been missing all this time. Now it was all she could think about. She shook her head and a few tendrils of hair slipped from the bun coiled tightly at the nape of her neck. She was an intelligent, driven, successful woman and she'd be damned if she'd ever follow his orders again—or go to work sans panties. What had she been thinking?

That you want this. You want the pleasure that comes with submission.

Okay, so it was true, and she'd own that truth without a hint of embarrassment. If she'd learned one thing from Quinn at his summer villa, it was that a submissive was strong because she surrendered her power willingly. There was no denying that she *did* want to give her body to him, to let him take control of her pleasure and her pain. Deep down she was a woman with deep-seated needs only a man like Quinn could satisfy.

A noise crawled out of her throat and she turned quickly, making sure her office door was shut. Fortunately it was late Friday and most of the office staff had cleared out for the weekend. The last thing she wanted was for anyone to know that she wasn't fully focused on her upcoming trial. Someday she'd like to make partner at the firm. Which meant she needed to get her mind off Quinn and back on her work, where it belonged.

Resolve firmly in place, Rebecca walked back to her desk and sat down, determined to get through her paperwork before she met her three best friends for drinks at Onyx, their favorite upscale cocktail bar two blocks away. They'd been dying to hear about her weekend at Freedom and they wouldn't be disappointed, even though she'd never made it to her final destination.

She was reaching for the file on her upcoming case when her phone pinged. She reached into her desk and pulled out her iPhone. Expecting it to be her friends questioning her whereabouts, she stole a quick glance at the screen. But when she saw Quinn's name, her heart jumped into her throat and the pen fell from her fingers.

Forgive me.

With shaky fingers she texted, *For what?*

I wanted to come sooner, but couldn't.

Even though she was feeling jilted, she didn't want to come across as high maintenance and needy so she texted back, *It's fine. I've been busy.*

She stared at the phone for a long time, waiting for him to text back. Despite the fact that she was upset with him for abandoning her, heat zinged through her body, setting off a series of explosions deep inside.

You're hurt.

She exhaled slowly and stared at the skyline outside her window. Damn it, she *was* hurt. And mad at him for ignoring her all week. And at herself for letting it matter enough to hurt. *I'm fine.*

No games, Rebecca. You need to be honest with me.

She'd done some research since coming home. Honesty was a very big part of the Dom/sub relationship, and the truth was, deep down she really was hurt. She'd waited all week to see him, to hear from him, and he hadn't so much as sent a follow-up text. Was she being foolish for feeling rejected— after all, they weren't in a committed relationship—or were her feelings justified?

The more she thought about it, the more it bothered her. She really liked Quinn, and while she had no problem giving him control of her body when they were together, she wasn't about to surrender everything to him, or forge anything deeper with him. Not that he had suggested a relationship other than physical. This thing between them really was just a game, and she had boundaries that were necessary to maintain for a reason. If life in foster care had taught her anything, it was to keep a measure of mental control and distance. *Low expectations, low disappointments.* After being tossed around from home to home, she knew all too well that once someone used her to get what they wanted, they were quick to discard her like yesterday's newspaper. *Never again.* She was a grown woman now, and no way would she ever set herself up for that kind of hurt again.

Are you there?

A knock sounded on her door, and she quickly texted back. *I have to go. Someone is at my door.*

She dropped her phone, climbed from her chair and took a moment to compose herself. Her shoes clicked on the tile floor and broke the quiet of her office as she made her way across the tile floor. She plastered on a smile and pulled her door open, but the second she saw Quinn standing there, his mere presence overwhelming the hallway—and her—she faltered backward.

"Whoa." He wrapped one strong arm around her waist. He pulled her to him and her body melted against his hardness as he looked at her with those dark, all-knowing eyes of his.

"What…what are you doing here?" She glanced past his broad shoulders, taking in the darkened corridor, wondering how he'd gotten through the building's tight security.

"How did you—?"

"All that matters is that I'm here now." He stepped farther into the room and shut the door behind him. The sound of the lock clicking into place sent shivers of anticipation skittering through her.

Struggling for a modicum of composure, she pushed from his arms and stepped back. Her gaze roamed over his chiseled face, then traveled downward, to the crisp white dress shirt that accentuated the breadth of his shoulders and muscular chest. Going lower to his black dress pants, she admired the way they hung on his waist and hugged him in all the right places. Her gaze tracked upward and when she met his glance, he angled his head, his eyes moving over her face.

"Rebecca?" He cupped her elbow and dragged her back into his embrace. When she blinked up at him, his eyes softened, and the hard angles in his face relaxed as he framed her face with his hands. The rough pad of his thumb brushed over her cheek. "Look at you. So needy for me," he said tenderly.

Heat moved into Rebecca's face. She hated that he was right, that she did indeed feel needy when she'd just sworn to remain emotionally uninvolved. "I'm not…it's not that," she shot back.

His hand slipped around her neck, his thumb brushing the base of her hairline as he held her still. "Never be ashamed of your wants," he said, his eyes hardening a little.

She squared her shoulders as his touch went right through her. "I'm not."

A beat of silence stood between them, and then, "I apologize for leaving you in such a state." His eyes darkened to nearly black, his voice several octaves deeper than it was moments ago. "I had an emergency that took me out of town."

She wanted to ask what the emergency was, where he'd gone and what he'd been doing, but she wasn't so sure she wanted to hear the answer, which, once again, set alarm bells jangling. She had no claims on him—nor did she want any.

His hands on the back of her neck tightened and he aligned his lips with hers like he was going to kiss her. "Otherwise nothing would have kept me from you. Nothing. You do understand that, don't you?"

Oh God, when he put it like that it was all she could do to stop herself from melting. The way he held her, looked at her, made her feel like the most important, most cherished woman in the world.

She nodded.

"Don't nod. Answer me."

"I understand," she said.

"Good." His mouth closed over hers, the warmth of his lips and the sweetness of his breath reminding her how much care there was in the lifestyle. He inched back. "I'm here now, kitten, and I plan to make up for neglecting you."

Kitten?

He hadn't given her a pet name before, and she had to admit, she kind of liked it. He turned his hand around and brushed his knuckles over her cheek, his eyes so focused on her, she was sure he could reach into her soul and see more than anyone else, which scared her a little. The last thing she wanted was for him to see the frightened little girl from her childhood and the demons that still haunted her.

"I've missed you." He gave her a little nudge, walking her backward toward the sofa near her window.

"Do you…do you go away often?"

He stopped and slanted his head, his eyes narrowing. He put his hands on her shoulders, turning her to face him directly. "What is it you want to know?"

"I guess I was just wondering where you were."

His palms slid down her arms, until they closed over her hands. "Come here." He guided her to the sofa, sat down and pulled her onto his lap. "Now tell me, what is it that has you so upset?"

In awe that he could read her so well, that she couldn't hide anything from him, she said, "I thought maybe you went to Freedom." That he'd found someone else to play with and was tossing her aside, like so many others had done in the past.

"And that would bother you?"

"No," she said quickly, not wanting to come off as insecure as she felt. "I…I was just disappointed…I'd been expecting to see you. I thought maybe you were done with…" She let her words fall off as his face softened with her honest admission.

"I was out of town visiting my mother," he explained.

"Oh." Okay, she hadn't expected that.

"She had a fall and I needed to be there for her."

Her heart hitched and she hated herself for thinking the worst about him. "Is she going to be okay?"

"She is."

Rebecca pictured him with his mother and looked down, feeling a pinch of loneliness. Having been abandoned by her mother when she was a toddler, she had no memories of her. A lump gathered in her throat, a tug of longing in her gut as she thought about his relationship with his mother. How she wanted what he had. His thumb slipped under her chin and he lifted her face until their eyes met.

"What is it?" he asked.

"Nothing. I just think it's nice."

"What else?" he asked, reading her like she was an open book.

"I just…I never knew my mother."

He paused, like he was waiting for her to continue, but she didn't want to travel down that road, not ever again. Reliving the nightmare of her early teen years, when her foster mother had locked her away in a dark, rat-infested basement for hours on end wasn't something she wanted anyone to know. There'd been no window in the dank, claustrophobic room, just disease-infested rodents—and her. Every sound, every fear was amplified without the sense of sight, and it had taken her full mental capacity to get through those days. She fought off a shiver and pushed those thoughts to the back of her mind, determined never to put herself in a situation where she'd experience something so horrific again.

When she pinched her lips tight, Quinn didn't press for more and for that she was grateful. Some things were too painful to share with another person, and better left buried in the past.

He finally broke the quiet and said, "You're under my care now, kitten. And I promise, you'll never feel alone or frightened again."

Something inside Rebecca's chest squeezed. She swallowed the lump pushing into her throat. When Quinn said things like that, it was so easy to forget this thing between them was only about sex. She'd be wise to remember, however, because soon enough, when he had his fill of her, he'd move on to someone else, which only gave credence to her logic to keep her emotional distance.

A noise sounded in the hall and unease moved through her as she looked toward her locked door. Quinn dipped a hand under the hem of her dress. The feel of his warm palm on her leg thrilled her. She'd only been with him one weekend but there was no denying that she'd missed his touch. Craved it.

His thumb and forefinger slipped between her closed legs, and he widened them to gain entry to the spot that needed him most. She inched her thighs open, giving him better access. His hand slid along her skin, barely touching, but making her aware of him all the same. Warm fingers climbed higher, and the softness on his face disappeared when he felt the silky barrier.

His nostrils flared and his voice took on a hard edge. "You haven't followed my instructions."

His thumb brushed her clit through her panties, and her eyes slipped shut as a moan caught in her throat. *God that feels good.* He quickly pulled his hand away and the movement pulled her thoughts back.

Her lids flew up. "Quinn…"

"Stand up."

Her knees wobbled slightly as she pushed off his lap and stood before him. "I told you when I come to you, I don't want you wearing panties."

"That was Monday," she shot back, having spent all week torn between wanting to obey and coveting the punishment that came with defiance. "I couldn't go all week without panties."

"I want you to be ready for me at all times."

"But—"

"Take them off."

"I don't think—"

"Rebecca," he said, holding his command as his eyes hardened.

"I did as you initially asked, but you can't expect me to go bare all week in the off chance that you decided to show up."

His shoulders squared, but she remained insolent, even though he wasn't a man who took disobedience lightly.

"Give them here." His tone was deeper, the warning clear.

"Fine," She peeled them off, scrunched them in her hand and took a step toward him. He held his hand out and she looked at it for a moment before giving in. He curled his palms around them and stuffed them into the front pocket of his dress pants. He leaned back, sinking into the sofa. "You remember what happens when you don't follow my rules, don't you?"

Her thoughts raced back to when he put her over his knee, the sting of his palm against her flesh, the burst of lust that had followed. She wanted that again. God help her, but she wanted it.

"Yes," she said.

He nodded as something passed over his eyes. His brow furrowed briefly, then smoothed out again. "It has occurred to me that you have so much to learn about the lifestyle."

She thought about the research she'd done. He was right. She had so much to learn. "Yes, I do." She looked down, a little uncertain. Her teeth scraped over her bottom lip, then her glance met his. "Will you teach me?"

A look she couldn't identify crossed his face, making her feel a little more tentative. He waved his hand over his lap. "All in good time, but first…"

She lifted her dress and, on her stomach, she laid over his lap, reveling in the feel of his warm hand caressing her backside. For a minute she thought he was just going to touch her, stroke her softly, but then the first hard smack came and she yelped in surprise and pleasure. She quickly clamped her hand over her mouth. Her door might be closed and locked but that didn't mean anyone still in their office down the hall couldn't hear her or know what was going on. He rubbed his hand over her ass, soothing the sting he left behind, then his palm came down again, a little more force behind it this time.

"Widen your legs."

She did so with pleasure, and the next strike hit her clit. *Yes...*

Quinn ran his fingers over the slope of her cheek, then dipped them between her legs. He brushed against her mound, coming perilously close to her swollen nub. He parted her with his fingers, and when he dipped into her liquid heat, he made a noise, something that sounded like a tortured growl.

"Wet," he said. "You really have missed me."

She bit her lip, wanting to beg for it, but knowing better than to ask. Of course, there was another way to show him what she wanted. She tipped her ass in the air to entice him, to tempt him to touch her.

"I know what you're doing." Smack. "And that's enough."

Oh God!

A moment passed, and he said, "Normally I wouldn't let you come, kitten. There is no reward for straying from my instructions, but since my unexpected absence has left you so needy, I could be convinced to change my mind."

"Please…" she murmured shamelessly. Wanting to entice him even more, she lifted her ass up higher, hoping to make him as crazed as she was, except he wasn't a man who lost control easily. In fact, she'd yet to see him come undone.

"Stay still," he commanded, and his hand came down again. Heat moved through her and she wondered what it would be like to be hit with something harder. A flogger on her backside would surely send her to subspace—a place where the world disappeared, and euphoria was reached. At least, what she'd read had promised something of that nature.

She stopped moving, and he gave her pussy a whack. She stifled a moan and tuned everything out. The sound of cars on the road below were now nothing but a distant buzz as she concentrated on the pleasure racing through her body. His finger found her clit, and he brushed it ever so gently as another finger dipped inside her. He pushed deep, and because her body had been so ready for his touch after a week of waiting, she knew she wouldn't last much longer.

She could feel his hardness pressing into her stomach and her mouth watered to taste him again, to feel him swell as she drew him to the back of her throat. He plunged deep, then drew his finger out, only to sink it inside again. Her heart raced, her skin came alive, and even though she wanted to buck against his hand, she held herself still, the way he'd taught her.

Infused with lust, she sucked in a quick breath, catching the tang of her arousal as it saturated the air. He applied more pressure to her clit and her muscles quivered.

"Poor kitten," he murmured as her body thrummed. He worked his finger faster, running the pad over the sensitive bundle inside, and her breath grew shallow. "Have you been touching yourself?" he asked.

"No," she said breathlessly. "I've been waiting."

"Such a good girl." A second finger joined the first, and her pussy squeezed around him. "I'll see to it that you're never left in such a state again."

"Quinn…" she cried out.

"Not yet, kitten. Not until I say."

Her body flared hot, the delicious pressure between her legs coming to a peak. He continued to stroke her and she concentrated on her breathing, to keep herself from tumbling over.

Her body rippled, need gripping her hard. Her fingernails raked over the leather sofa, then curled into fists.

"One more second, kitten. Just one more."

She made a whimpering sound, the intensity in his touch taking her higher and higher, until her vision blurred and nothing existed but this man and the way he was touching her. Reaching for control, she bit down on her lip.

"Come for me."

"Yes!" Her muscles clamped hard around his fingers as she tumbled into an orgasm so powerful it stole the breath from her lungs. Pleasure swept through her, pulling all her focus. Quinn kept his hands between her legs, drawing out her orgasm, and when her pussy finally stopped quaking, she sucked in a breath, trying to refill her lungs. She unfurled her damp fingers, stretched like a cat, and pressed them into the soft leather.

With unhurried movements, he trailed his wet fingers over her inner thighs and pulled her dress down to cover her bare ass.

"Come here," he said.

Pressing her palms into the soft leather, Rebecca pushed up. Her arms trembled under the weight of her upper body. She wobbled there for a second, but Quinn's hands were there, helping her up and onto his lap. She was drained, physically and emotionally. Drawing her knees up, she cuddled into him, pressing her face into his neck and drawing from his strength.

His thumb brushed her hair behind her ear. "Come home with me."

Rebecca pulled back and her mouth parted as she looked up at him. From the expression on his face, he appeared as surprised by the request as she was. "I...I..."

He cleared his throat and tightened his arms around her. "It's not a suggestion, kitten. My absence has been hard on you, and I want to give you the care you need."

She nodded, and absorbed his sensual warmth. "Okay, I just have to let my friends know. They're expecting me."

One brow arched. "These are the friends that sent you on a trip to Freedom?"

"Yes. They're foaming at the mouth to hear how my trip went."

"And what will you tell them?"

"That it will have to wait until tomorrow, because tonight I'm going to be with you."

His hand stilled on her face. "I won't keep you from your friends, but there are some things we need to discuss, sooner rather than later. Especially if I'm going to take you to Freedom, so we can explore your deeper needs."

"You want to take me to Freedom?"

"Of course, if you're in this, then you're in it all the way. There will be no middle of the road for me, understand?"

"Yes."

"Good, but first we need to go over your limits. If I'm going to take you down a path to full sensual freedom and properly care for you, then I need to know your boundaries and just how far you're willing to be pushed." She considered the research she'd done on limits and nodded. "Know this—I'll respect your limits, but I'll take you to the very edge, and then push you just a little farther. Only then will you experience the true and complete freedom of submitting."

She'd had a taste and wanted to know more, but the way he was looking at her spoke of full mental surrender and that was something she couldn't...*wouldn't* do. She was a strong woman, but could she really do this and keep her personal and professional life separate from the D/s lifestyle she was so curious about? She tossed that around for a while, then settled on yes, she could hold her own independence.

"Rebecca?"

Two

Quinn saw the flicker of uncertainty in Rebecca's big blue eyes at the mention of boundaries. Fierce protectiveness moved through him, because the last thing he wanted was for her to fear him, or her deeper needs. As she shied away from his gaze, he clenched down hard enough to break teeth. The muscles along his jaw ticked as he gave further consideration to her moment of hesitation.

Everyone had limits, yes, but he didn't want fear holding her back. No, he wanted—needed—her to give herself over to him completely, body and mind. He brushed his hand over his face and tapped his finger on his chin. He could understand her need to cling to control in her personal life. He admired her for it and would be sure to ease her into the lifestyle carefully. Good thing he was a patient man.

But a relationship with her, or any woman outside of sex, wasn't in the cards for him. Thanks to three generations of unfaithful Montgomery men who'd thrived on infidelity, neither Quinn nor his three brothers had been inclined to enter into a serious relationship. Better off to remain uncommitted than to risk that the *asshole* gene had trickled down the genetic bloodline to them.

He didn't want to be that guy, so he satisfied his needs in the dungeon and returned to his Manhattan home sexually sated and alone.

Always alone.

He'd never asked any woman to come home with him. Until tonight.

The question was, why? Why now? Why her? It went against his rules. Rules he had carefully put in place to protect not only himself from becoming a typical womanizing Montgomery, but to assure he never caused a woman the pain and heartache he'd watched his mother, and other Montgomery women, suffer.

Quinn rose from Rebecca's leather sofa and pulled her up with him, sliding his hand around her body to rest at the small of her back. Slipping his thumb under her chin, he tipped her mouth up. Her lips parted and she made a breathy little sound as her eyes fell shut.

Surrender. Sweet and pure.

For him.

This. This was what drove him to rip down his rules, shred them to pieces and take the risk. The driving need to capture, claim and possess pulled at him with a force he'd never felt before, leaving him shaken and raw.

"Look at me."

She did as requested, her eyes round with uncertainty. His gaze moved over her face and the almost frightened way she looked at him.

"Quinn?" she asked as he continued to stare at her.

"You do know you have nothing to fear, right?"

"I know. It's just that…this is all so new to me."

"And my promise to you is that I will never let anything happen that you're not ready for." She relaxed in his arms, and when her phone pinged, he looked at her desk. "Your friends?"

"Probably. They're at Onyx waiting for me. I was supposed to meet them after work."

"Perhaps I should meet them before we go away for the weekend."

A smile touched her mouth. "You want to meet them?"

"Of course. Friends are important and I want yours to meet me and get to know me so they know you're in good hands when we go away together."

That brought a smile to her face. She stepped from the circle of his arms and walked to her desk. "I think you'll really like them."

"I know I will."

She fished her purse from her bottom drawer and picked her phone up. Quinn put his hands in his pockets and rocked on his feet as her fingers raced over her screen. When she looked back up at him with equal measures of anticipation and nervousness, he stepped toward her, wanting to reassure her that she was in capable hands.

"Ready?" he asked.

He guided her into the hall, and in an office nearby he could hear someone chatting on the phone. Rebecca turned in the direction of the sound, then back to Quinn. She gave him an apologetic look.

"We keep late hours."

In an attempt to lighten her mood, he said, "Believe me, I know just how hard you work. I was on the opposing team once, remember?"

She cringed. "Right."

"That's all you have to say?" he teased. "If you weren't so good at what you do my company wouldn't have had to fork over hundreds of thousands of dollars."

"I think I'm going to take that as a compliment."

"You should. It was meant to be one. I admire your dedication and that smart brain of yours." She beamed at the compliment.

"My friends think I need to loosen up and live a little more. That's why they gave me the ticket to Freedom."

Her friends were right. Quinn knew all about working hard, but he also knew how to balance that with playtime—something Rebecca desperately needed to learn. He took in her flushed cheeks as they made their way to the elevator. He stabbed the "down" button.

She pushed her hair off her shoulders as they entered the elevator, and the sweet scent of berries reached his nostrils. His cock hardened, and, for a moment, he considered taking her right there against the back wall. But he needed to slow things down with her and introduce her carefully.

She was strong, yes, but there was a vulnerably beneath the surface, one she went to great lengths to hide. It was that vulnerability that brought out the protector in him. When he'd whisked her away to his summer villa last week, it had been with the intention to awaken her submissive side, but she'd also unleashed something in him, and he knew he had to have her in his life. Being away from her this week had been as hard for him as it seemed to be for her. But now that he was back, he had no intentions of letting her out of his sight.

The elevator doors shut behind them, and he pulled her close, his mouth thinning as her body tensed against his. Her vulnerabilities had returned when his only wish was to put her at ease. "This weekend I'll take you to Freedom, but you won't be playing," he said quietly.

"No?"

"No, it will be the beginning of your training period."

Disappointment moved over her face. "Oh."

He skimmed his fingers down the length of her arm. "It's not a race, kitten. I want to take my time with you, introduce you properly, but this weekend I'm signed on to be Dungeon Master."

Rebecca suddenly turned in his arms, her lower lip caught between her teeth, her eyes bright with excitement as she gazed up at him. "I did some research while you were gone."

Something swelled in Quinn's chest. Pleasure? Pride? He wasn't sure, since it was unlike anything he'd ever felt before, but that she'd taken the time to learn more about the lifestyle moved him. Unfortunately, while the Internet was full of valuable information, it was also bloated with inaccurate instruction. Every dungeon was run differently, depending on who was in charge. Quinn made sure to play only in those that followed his own personal and moral code. Since her wellbeing was his utmost concern as she learned, he'd settle for nothing less for Rebecca, as well.

The elevator opened and they stepped off. "What exactly is Dungeon Master?" she queried quietly as she stepped up to the counter to sign out. The night attendant handed her a clipboard and she scratched her name down. Then she handed the pen to Quinn. He signed out and slid the pen and clipboard across the marble counter.

"Good night, Tim," he said.

"Have a safe weekend." Tim presented a mask of professionalism as he pressed a button under the desk.

Rebecca eyed Quinn. "Wait, what was that all about?"

Quinn smiled, pushed open the heavy glass front door and gestured for her to exit. "Tim is a friend."

Her steps slowed and, as her eyes adjusted to the dark outside, she glanced back into the building. "Is he…?"

"Privacy is always respected."

"Oh," she said, then mumbled something about that's how he must have gotten into the building.

They turned the corner and walked down the bustling sidewalk, making their way to Onyx.

"Speaking of privacy, are you allowed to talk about the duties of a Dungeon Master?

He nodded. "I'll be responsible for overseeing the other Doms when they take their subs into a scene. To make sure rules are being abided by and everyone's safety is being adhered to."

"What happens if the rules are broken?"

"The Dom will be shown the door. I don't take that kind of thing lightly."

"How did you get into the lifestyle?"

They maneuvered their way through the crowds. Quinn touched her back to move her in front of him as they sidestepped a group of rowdy teens. He stopped and picked up a potato chip bag and dropped it into the trashcan. "I always felt unsatisfied, like something was lacking in my relationships. One night a college girlfriend suggested we go to a club. The instant I entered, took in a few of the scenes, I knew what had been missing from my life."

Rebecca nodded, and from the expression on her face, Quinn imagined she was recalling the enlightenment she'd experienced with him on the island. "So, while you're busy with your duties as Dungeon Master, what will I be doing?"

"Watching," he said. "Learning."

They stopped at the traffic light. The *Walk* hand showed and they crossed the street. When they reached Onyx, Quinn pulled the heavy black door open and again placed his hand on her back to guide her in.

She looked up at him, uncertainty in her eyes. "Will I be on my own?"

The noise level increased as they stepped inside the darkened lounge. He put his mouth close to her ear and explained. "Never. You'll stay by my side and wear my bracelet, which will let the other Doms know that you're mine. I think watching is the best way to understand, see what interests you or not, to know your limits. Sometimes we can agree or disagree to things on paper, but then when we see scenes being played out, see the reality in the act, it can change how both the Dom and the sub feel. Your hard limit might become soft and vice versa."

He felt a shiver move through her, and then he heard her friends calling out to her. "There they are." She pointed to a table with three women waving her over.

Rebecca appeared a little more anxious than moments ago as she weaved through the crowd toward her friends. Quinn followed her, watching three sets of eyes go from Rebecca to him. They studied him like a bug under a microscope.

These women were very protective of her and wouldn't hesitate to relieve him of his balls if he hurt her. Resisting the urge to cup himself, he pulled her chair out and watched her relax in their presence.

"This is Quinn Montgomery," she said. "Quinn this is Melanie, Lillian and Sophie."

"Ladies." He made a point of looking each one in the eye. They stared back, unblinking. One drummed blood-red nails on the tabletop. Well, hell. Did his balls just draw up a little? "What are you all drinking?"

"Martinis," they all said in unison.

"Gin," Melanie added.

"Then I'll be back with four." He put his mouth close to Rebecca's ear. "I'm sure you need a minute or two alone with your friends." He turned to leave, but before he could even take one step, he heard the questions flying. He chuckled to himself, instantly liking her friends and their loyalty to Rebecca.

Quinn stepped up to the bar and ordered four martinis and a scotch on the rocks. He placed the drinks on a tray and carried them to the table. When he arrived, he met with silence. Again, all eyes fell on him, Rebecca's included. He handed out the drinks, then reached for an empty chair at the neighboring table and put it beside Rebecca's.

"So," Melanie asked, running her hand along the stem of her glassware, "do you have any brothers?"

"Mel," Rebecca said, looking mortified while her other friends laughed.

Quinn put his hand on the back of Rebecca's chair and lightly brushed her shoulder to relax her. "As a matter of fact, I do." Quinn swirled the amber liquid in his glass before taking a drink and setting it back on the table. "Three, in fact."

"Oh, I didn't realize." Rebecca looked at him. "You never mentioned that."

Her friend Melanie mumbled something about him being too preoccupied with other things to talk, and the other two murmured their agreement.

Giving all his focus to Rebecca, he nodded. "They live in L.A., and Melanie is right, when I'm with you I'm not thinking about my brothers." He turned to Melanie. "How about you, Melanie? Do you have siblings?"

Melanie fished an olive from her glass and eased in into her mouth. "Yes, but I want to hear more about these brothers of yours. Do they visit often?"

Quinn laughed. "Not as often as I'd like."

Her friend Sophie sat up straighter, her expression serious. "Your family is very important to you. You care about them greatly."

He nodded and narrowed his eyes, scrutinizing her. "Yes. I'd do anything for them."

She picked up her glass, her gaze never leaving his. "Same," she said over the rim before she took a drink.

Soon enough they fell into easy conversation, discussing work, family and their weekend plans. He neglected to mention that he'd be taking Rebecca out of town, only that she'd be spending her time with him. If she wanted to fill them in on what they did behind closed doors, that was up to her. A while later, after finishing off the last of his drink, Quinn glanced at his watch, anxious to have Rebecca all to himself.

When their banter finally ended, he turned to Rebecca. "Shall we?" When she nodded, he pushed from his chair and reached for her hand. He looked at her friends. "You ladies don't mind if I keep her to myself this weekend, do you?"

"Hell no," Melanie said while Lilliana and Sophie grinned up at him.

"See you later," Rebecca said.

"Twelve is the magic number," Melanie called after her as Quinn put his hand on her back to guide her out.

"Twelve?" he asked.

Rebecca opened her mouth as if to speak, then buried her face in her hands. "When they sent me to Freedom, Melanie told me not to come back until I had twelve orgasms."

"Ah, I see." He guided her outside and the heat of the night fell over them. "Did you keep up your end of the bargain?" He pulled his phone from his pocket and sent a message. When finished, he drew Rebecca in to his arms.

She poked him in the chest. "*You* kept up that end of the bargain."

He laughed, a deep, hearty laugh that pulled a smile from her. "I like your friends."

"They like you too."

"Although I'm not too sure if either of my brothers could handle Melanie."

"She's all bark and no bite," Rebecca explained. She wobbled a little in her heels. "Whoa, I think that one drink went straight to my head."

"You've not had dinner," he stated, planning to rectify that.

The driver pulled up to the curb and Quinn opened the back door to let her in. He slid in beside her and noticed the way she was looking around the limo. He couldn't stop the swell of pride that filled his chest at her wide-eyed appreciation.

He leaned back in his seat and heard Rebecca's stomach rumble. "I was thinking I'd cook for you at my place, but now I'm wondering if we should pick something up."

"You like to cook?"

He moved closer to her and put his hand on her leg. "I like to do a lot of things."

Her lips quivered as she sucked in a breath. "Yes, well, I guess I have a lot to learn about you."

"And about yourself."

The driver pulled up in front of his home, and Quinn opened his door. He reached for Rebecca and she shimmied across the seat. He grabbed her hand and helped her out.

"This place is as beautiful as your summer estate," she said.

"I'm glad you approve." They stepped inside and were greeted by Eloise, the woman who oversaw his staff and the care of his home.

"Quinn," she greeted cheerily, her eyes lighting with her smile.

"Eloise, this is Rebecca. Rebecca, this is Eloise. She takes care of everything around here. I'd be lost without her."

The two exchanged pleasantries, then he said, "Tell the staff they have the night off. I'll be cooking tonight."

Eloise smiled at Quinn. "Very well."

He pulled two tickets from his pocket. "Why don't you and Frederick take the weekend off? I won't be around, anyway."

Her eyes widened as she looked at the Broadway tickets. "*The Phantom of the Opera*. I've been wanting to go."

"I know."

After dismissing Eloise, Quinn turned his attention to Rebecca. He took her hand and led her down the long hall toward his office.

"You're very good to your staff," she said quietly.

He stopped in the doorway and turned her to him. "I take care of those in my charge, Rebecca. Don't ever forget that."

Heat moved into her face. She nodded and when he stepped to the side to wave her into his office, she pushed past him. Quinn went to his desk and turned on his computer. He watched Rebecca move around his private space, looking at this, touching that, as the computer went through the process of booting up. She stopped at his bookshelf.

"You have a wide range of interests." She ran her fingers over his books.

He watched her a moment longer. As she touched his belongings, he pulled up the file containing the contract and sent it to the printer. Giving the machine time to do its thing, he rounded the desk and stepped up behind her. "Right now I'm only interested in you." He put his lips on her neck and kissed gently.

He felt her shiver beneath his mouth. His cock hardened at the images of her bound and blindfolded, mouth open and legs spread for him. She tipped her head to the side and gave him better access to her neck, making him want to take her hard and fast against the bookshelf. But he wouldn't. Didn't want to risk the progress he'd made so far. He gave her a final kiss on the neck and stepped away, going to his desk and taking the contract off the printer.

"What's that?" she asked.

"Come with me and I'll explain." He took her hand. They made their way to the kitchen and he gestured for her to sit at the long, granite-topped island. He dropped the papers onto the countertop and slid them to her, then went to work on loosening the top two buttons on his shirt and rolling up his sleeves. "Do you know what high protocol is?"

"It's when a sub addresses a Dom as 'sir' at all times."

"Yes, among other things, but for now that's all it will be between us. It's used to strengthen the Dom/sub relationship. There will be times when I'll want you to follow high protocol while in the dungeon and times I won't. When outside of the dungeon, I will never ask you to follow high protocol."

"You said I would wear a bracelet."

He smiled, happy she was asking questions. "Yes, and it's to signify that you're a novice and that you are hands-off."

Her eyes glimmered with sensuality as she looked at him, hanging on his every word. He couldn't help but grin. Her eagerness to please him shone in the depths of her eyes. It was that eagerness that would make her the perfect pupil. He pulled lettuce, tomato, cucumber and radish from the crisper and placed them on the counter. "Do you know what hard and soft limits are?"

A few loose tendrils of hair fell from the bun on her head as she leaned forward and scanned the paper. She grabbed the wisps and wrapped them around her finger. "I think so."

"A hard limit is something you will not do because it goes against your moral code, or you simply don't like it, or don't have any interest in it." She looked up at him and he continued, "A soft limit is something you might not want to do right now, but it's possible you'll consider it in the future. You will also see a list of props and a pain scale." She nodded and continued to scan the paper. "Pain is a big deal. What you perceive as the highest level you can tolerate may change. You must use your safe word if you find it too much."

"Okay," she said.

"Next to the props you can check the box for *Won't object, Maybe*, or *Not interested*," he continued. "Whatever you choose will be respected."

From across the island, Quinn watched the rise and fall of Rebecca's chest as her breathing changed. The idea of the dungeon and all that awaited within it excited her.

"Look this over, and ask as many questions as you need. I don't want you to check off any boxes just yet, or make comments until you've actually been in a dungeon. I just want you to look at this and spend some time thinking about it."

As she scanned the papers, he took two steaks from the fridge and walked outside to light the barbecue. When he came back in, Rebecca was engrossed in the contract. He watched the way her eyes widened with interest, or her brows furrowed as she read something that gave her pause, like now, when she tapped her finger on a particular section.

"I don't think I'd be interested in breath play or hot wax, and especially not blood play." She looked up at him as he washed the produce. "Have you ever…?"

"I'm open to many new experiences, but blood play isn't something I'm interested in. Even if it was, if it's a hard limit for you, I'd never ask you to participate."

She nodded, obviously relieved, and returned her attention to the contract.

Quinn stepped out to put the steaks on the grill. He came back in and put the vegetables on the cutting board. When he cast her another look, something akin to fear dimmed her eyes. His heart raced, and he pushed the cutting board aside.

"Rebecca?"

"Yes…" she said, sounding a little breathless.

"Look at me."

Her eyes lifted, but she seemed to be looking through him, not at him.

"What is it?" he persisted.

Her gaze fell back to the contract. "I was looking at…"

Quinn tried to pull the paper around to see what had her so upset, but Rebecca held it firmly in place. "The pain scale?" he asked.

"No, the props."

"You don't think you'd like to use props?"

"Yes, no…"

"Is it yes or no?" He laid his hand over hers. "I need you to be honest with me, but more importantly, you have to be honest with yourself."

She let out a breath and her hand loosened on the paper.

"I could never be blindfolded." The words came out in a rush. He waited a moment, but she didn't say anything else. To be blindfolded had everything to do with trust and freeing oneself mentally. The blindfold was one of his favorite props, allowing his sub to tune out everything else around her and focus only on the pleasure he was offering. But some found it scary being inside their own head, where fears and demons dwelled. However, when one was forced to concentrate on senses and emotions when they couldn't see, it could heighten the whole experience for both parties playing.

He leaned across the counter and touched her face. "What is it about the blindfold that scares you?"

She opened her mouth, only to close it again. A beat passed and she said, "It's just not something I'm interested in."

He wanted to probe, push her to give him a real answer, but decided to let it go for now. Whatever it was that lived in her psyche and had spooked her, ran deep, very deep. It would take a careful, patient hand to help her let go of it.

"Then you will mark that as not interested. Again, it's something that can be changed if you choose to later."

She visibly relaxed. "Okay."

"You can make amendments later, if need be," he said, appealing to the attorney in her.

"I won't be."

He gave her hand a reassuring squeeze and leaned back. Even though he wanted to know what had happened to make her fear being blindfolded, now wasn't the time to press for reasons. That would take trust, and building trust would take time. "That's enough for tonight. Let's eat."

The relief in her eyes almost killed him. He pointed to his wine rack. "Why don't you pick out a bottle of wine while I take care of the steaks.

Her mood changed quickly, and her eyes flared as they met his. "Are you trying to get me tipsy?"

"Never," he said. "When I touch your body, I want you fully aware of what's happening and that it's me doing it."

Her eyes glazed over with lust, and to keep from dragging her across the counter and taking her on the cold, hard granite, he went outside to check on the steaks. A few minutes later, he came back inside to find her sipping a glass of red wine. He picked up the bottle and read the label. "Good choice."

He placed their steaks on plates, then divvied up the salad. While he would have preferred to skip dinner altogether, she needed to eat, especially with what he had planned for tonight.

"Your brothers," she began, picking up her fork. "Are they…? Do they…?"

"Yes," he said. "We're all into the lifestyle. Two are Doms, one is a sub."

Her head came back with a start. "I guess I never really thought of a man as a sub."

"Don't get me wrong, he's alpha in every way, but he likes to be taken to his knees in the dungeon."

She put a piece of steak in her mouth and chewed quietly. Was she visualizing herself on her knees, in front of him? He sure as hell hoped so, because that's where his thoughts had instantly traveled.

She reached for her wine and took a sip, then her eyes widened as though she'd had an epiphany. "Maybe he'd be the one for Melanie."

He cleared his throat. Truthfully, he seemed more suited for Sophie. Instinct told him she was a woman who'd like to take charge. "Rebecca?"

"Yes."

"I don't want to talk about my brothers, or your friends."

She blinked. "Oh, okay. What do you want to talk about?"

"I don't want to talk. In fact, I want you to finish your meal so I can tie you to my bed." Christ, he knew she needed to eat, but he ached to have her at his mercy.

Eyes full of want shot to his as an erotic little whimper bubbled in the depths of her throat. He forced a piece of steak into his mouth and chewed while he nodded to her plate, a suggestion she do the same.

She dug into her salad, and sexual energy arced between them as they ate. Christ, they were creating enough electricity to light up a city block. When over half her meal was gone, he pushed his plate away and stood. He walked to his bar, poured them each an after-dinner brandy and handed one to her, wanting to taste the sweetness of it on her lips when he kissed her.

She took a small sip and he leaned in to lick a drop from her lower lip. She moaned, and he reached for her hand.

"Come with me." Heat hummed between them as they walked to his room. He pushed the door open and stepped back, waiting for her to enter. She stepped into the room and looked around. "Make yourself comfortable," he said, taking a sip of his drink before he put it on the nightstand.

She walked over to his dresser and ran her fingers along the mahogany. She turned toward the bed. Color bloomed on her cheeks as she touched the bedposts, ones he'd soon have her tied to.

"Your furniture is beautiful."

His eyes moved over her. "I enjoy being surrounded by beautiful things."

"Did you pick it out?"

"I did."

She ran one hand up one of the thick posts and back down again. Quinn swallowed a groan. For a moment he thought it was an innocent action, that she had no idea she was mimicking a hand job, but when he caught the slight grin pulling at her mouth, he shook his head. Such a bad girl.

"That's enough." He stepped up to her to remove her drink. He placed it on the table beside his, then turned back to her.

Her eyes widened with innocence. "What?"

"You know what. And if you keep that up, you'll find yourself over my knees."

"Sorry, sir," she said.

Sir. Such a small word, one his former subs had spoken more times than he cared to count. He always experienced a measure of satisfaction in hearing it the first time, but the breathy sound of it on Rebecca's lips stroked his ears as well as his cock. Then she dropped to her knees before him, legs parted, hands on her thighs, her head bent in submission. Something stirred in his chest. Pride? Yes, there was always that moment, that rush of sexual energy at achieving dominance, but this…this was different, an alien sensation he'd never achieved with a submissive before.

And it scared the hell out of him.

A surge of possession hit hard. "Who taught you to do this?" The thought of her kneeling before another man didn't set well with him. He pulled the clip from her hair, letting it fall down her back. He grabbed a handful, wrapped it around his hand three times, and tugged until their eyes met.

"Research," she said. "Am I doing it right?"

His heart nearly stopped. She'd done research…to please him. He should be careful, because he liked that too much. "It's perfect," he assured her. Jesus, *she* was perfect. He swallowed and composed himself. It was getting personal, something he couldn't afford to let happen.

She smiled and he couldn't help but think she might be ready sooner than he'd expected.

"I want to please you."

"You are. You do." She was a natural, not programmed in her responses like those he usually played with, and it did something to him, something that made him feel peculiar inside. He leaned down and pressed his lips to hers, enjoying the flavor of brandy on her tongue as it swept out and met his. He went deeper, until he tasted only Rebecca, the girl who was getting to him in a way no other ever had.

He let go of her hair and her head fell forward, her mouth inches from his cock. Her tongue slid across her bottom lip and it took all his strength not to shove down his pants, pull out his cock and fuck her mouth six ways to Sunday.

"I want to feel this lovely mouth suck me off," he said, his voice deceptively level as his cock pushed against his zipper, draining the blood from his brain and damn near rendering him senseless. "Would you like that?"

She nodded.

"Use your words, Rebecca. I won't say it again."

"Yes, sir."

Fuck.

He flicked the button at his waistband open and pulled his zipper down. As he shoved his pants past his thighs, his cock sprang free and smacked Rebecca on the mouth.

Her head jerked back, and her eyes opened wide. "Sorry, kitten." He gave her an unapologetic grin. "But this is what you do to me."

Her grin told him how much that pleased her. She licked her lips, her eyes focused on his, and since this was her first time on her knees before him, he decided to cut her some slack. After all, she was trying very hard to please him and get in the right headspace for her training.

"Eyes lower," he reminded her. She looked down, and he said. "Open your mouth." She did as she was told and he brushed her hair behind her ears so he could watch as he fed her his cock. She went to reach for him, but he stopped her. "Hands stay on your knees."

"Yes, sir."

She put her hands back and he gripped the base of his cock. "A little wider, kitten." She opened her mouth until it formed a pretty little *O*, and he stepped closer, serving her his crown. Her tongue snaked out to lick a drop of pre-come, and the second he felt her wet heat, he fisted her hair and stifled a groan. She moved her head, trying to take more of him in, and he tugged on her hair to control her movements.

She made an impatient, whimpering sound, but it was replaced by a moan when he gave her another inch. Closing her mouth around him, she sucked hard, drawing him in deeper. Dammit, she was not the one in charge here, and if she didn't stop trying to take control, he was definitely going to put her over his knee.

Testing her, he pushed in deeper, until his head hit the back of her throat. She made a slight choking noise and he pulled back.

"Very good," he said, growing even harder at how deep she could take him. She sat up a bit straighter under his praise. She liked the encouragement. He'd remember that.

"Keep still." He began to power his hips forward, taking full control as he fucked her mouth. He fisted her hair tighter, preventing her from swaying with him, and when her breathing changed, he could tell how much she liked it. "Such a good little sub."

Her tongue raced over him, and pressure began brewing, but he had no intention of releasing in her mouth. No, he needed her tied and writhing on the bed beneath him. He pumped a few more times, his balls drawing tight to his body as his cock throbbed. There was something undeniably sexy in the way she took him into her mouth, something that turned him from a cultured man to a primal animal. His lids drifted down as he savored the sweetness of her mouth, letting the fire raging inside overtake him.

He began to sweat. Sweating, for Christ's sake. He shook his head to get it back on straight. Losing himself like this—from a *simple* blowjob—was completely out of character for him. Then again, he was beginning to believe there was nothing simple between them.

"Enough," he bit out.

He drew his cock out and lifted her to her feet. Her eyes were glazed with lust, and when he saw the wet circle around her lips, he almost shot off then and there. He backed her up until her knees hit the bed, then reached behind her to lower her zipper. The sound cut through the quiet as he held her gaze.

Her dress fell and she stood before him in nothing but a lace bra and her heels. Christ, the woman had a body that made a man want to corrupt her.

"Undress." She went to kick off the heels, but he stopped her. "The shoes stay." She nodded and slipped a hand around her back to free her bra. Her nipples hardened beneath his gaze, and it pleased him that he could arouse her from a look alone. He brushed the backs of his knuckles over her cheek, then ran his thumbs over her nipples. Her gaze fell away.

"Look at me when I touch you."

She focused on his face, and the need—for him—swimming in those big pools of blue had possession racing through him. "I have a gift for you," he said.

Her eyes widened in surprise. "You do?"

He reached into his nightstand, grabbed a box and handed it to her.

She removed the lid and pulled out two silk scarfs. A smile, sweet and genuine, curved her lips. She rubbed the soft fabric against her cheeks and all he could think about was how she'd look with them wrapped around her wrists, confining her to his bed.

"I picked them up when I was away."

"You were thinking of me," she said quietly.

"Of course I was. I thought you might like them."

"I do. They're beautiful." She looked up at him. "No guy has ever given me a gift, just for the sake of giving."

"Then maybe you've been with the wrong guys."

He fingered the soft silk, rubbing it between his thumb and index fingers. "I know we haven't gone over your limits yet, but if you agree, I'd like to tie you to my bed with these."

She glanced at the bedposts and wrapped the silk scarf around her fingers. "Do you…"

"Do I what?"

"Do you always tie your subs to your bed?"

Asking about what he did with other subs went against proper etiquette, but she was new to the lifestyle and it reminded him that with her, breaking rules was getting to be a habit.

Instead of answering, because he wasn't sure he was ready to admit that, to her or to himself, he looked at the scarves in her hand and said, "Yes or no."

Her long throat made a noise as she swallowed, the heat in her eyes telling him so much about her as she held the silk out to him.

He looked at the scarves, and then back at her. "I take that as a yes. But I need to hear you say it."

"Yes." She gathered the silk into his hands.

"What is your safe word?" he asked.

"Freedom."

He'd given her that word when he'd taken her to his summer villa and saw no need to change it now. "Say it again."

"Freedom."

"Don't ever hesitate to use it."

"I won't." She brushed the silk over her face. "So this was your plan all along. To give me this sexy gift after you lured me back to your place."

"Lured?"

She laughed. "You had every intention of tying me up and having your way with me."

He nudged her backward until she fell onto the bed. "Of course I did."

She propped herself up on her elbow, her beautiful body beckoning his mouth. "What would you have done if I hadn't agreed to come?"

He kneeled on the bed and slipped his hands under her waist to position her in the middle of the bed. "Then you would have left me with no choice."

"No choice?"

He slid off the bed, lifted her right arm and tied it to the post, testing the space with two fingers. Sometimes silk tightened and he needed to keep a close eye on her circulation. "That's right." He crossed the foot of the bed to reach her other side. She placed her arm over her head and he wrapped the silk around it. He grinned at her, his thoughts going back to when he'd whisked her away to his summer villa instead of flying her to the sex resort. "No choice but to kidnap you again."

Three

Her entire body quivered as she recalled the last time he'd pseudo-kidnapped her, and the way he'd nurtured her budding needs into full blossom.

The soft silk scarves brushed over her flesh and she could feel the strength and power in his touch as he secured her to the thick mahogany posts. While she should be afraid, after all, she'd never let a man restrain her before, this was Quinn, and she had nothing to fear from him.

After tying her to the bed, he stood back, hands on his hips, admiring his handy work, an air of command about him. A new intensity lit his eyes, one that filled her with equal amounts of anticipation and unease.

What did he see when he looked at her? A naked woman sprawled wide and restrained, his to do with as he pleased? She gave a little tug on the scarves, suddenly not a hundred percent sure about this anymore. Like Quinn had said, sometimes limits could change after watching a scene being played out. Except she wasn't watching, she was smack dab in the middle of it.

His dark, passion-imbued gaze moved over her body as he rid himself of his clothes. Her breath grew shallow as she took in his nakedness, the hardness of his cock as it strained to reach her. He was so beautiful, toned, tight and athletic. With unhurried movements, he moved between her legs. He slid a hand between her thighs to widen them more, and she moved beneath him, struggling against the binding.

"Stop moving or I'll restrain your legs as well."

She stilled instantly, responding to the command in his tone, and looked into his eyes for reassurance. Her heart stuttered, because behind the heat and lust, she spotted something else, something that spoke of a deeper need—for her. God, the way he looked at her, like no other woman in the world existed, warmed her blood.

Looking wild and untamed, he lightly tapped her pussy, and as she got her head into the game, she knew his touch was meant to arouse, not harm. Relaxing into his play, she stilled and waited to see what he'd do next.

He didn't disappoint.

At the foot of the bed, he widened her legs even farther, opening her up to him. Her entire body tightened in anticipation, waiting for his tongue to touch the place that needed him most. He pulled his hand back, leaving cold where there once was heat.

"Please…" she said, unable to stop herself. "Touch me."

He stroked her legs, his grin carnal, almost sinful when he stretched her lips with his fingers.

"Yessss," she hissed.

She resisted the urge to writhe, knowing any sort of movement would only slow him down, but there was nothing she could do to bite back the moan rising in her throat.

"Shh," he ordered. "No more talking."

Even though she wanted to scream, to ask him to just take her, she lay perfectly still. Like a marionette at its master's mercy, she waited for him to pull her strings. Despite his orders to remain motionless, there was no denying that following his instructions came with its own pleasures. He took his time, lightly touching her, stroking and caressing her pussy, everywhere and anywhere but her clit. God it ached to be suckled by his mouth, nibbled on with his teeth.

"It was wrong of me to leave you in such a state all week."

Her throat tightened, the torment on his face telling her it had pained him just as much as it had her. She pulled on her bindings, wanting to palm his muscles, but her thought disintegrated when he leaned forward and swiped his tongue over her clit.

Yesss....

"Is this what you've been waiting for?" She opened her mouth and then closed it again, remembering the rules and wondering if he was testing her. A slow smile tugged at his mouth. "You may speak."

"Yes," she murmured.

His hand trailed up her stomach to stimulate her sensitized nipples. Her pussy throbbed, desperate for something to clench around. Heat flashed between them and danced along her nerve endings, an ache unlike anything she'd ever experienced growing between her legs.

He snatched his glass of brandy off the nightstand and took a mouthful before positioning it between her breasts. He tilted the glass and the cool liquid splashed against her skin. She gasped as it pooled in the hollow of her breastbone and slowly dripped toward her pelvis.

It tickled her flesh, and her breath grew shallow. Quinn watched the stream, his eyes glued to it as his nostrils flared.

"Quinn…" she pleaded.

"Hush now." His voice was soft, but the muscles rippled along his strong jaw like he was clenching. He was all strength and power, like an animal pulling at its tether. A delicious shiver moved through her. She looked at his sensuous mouth, and the heat smoldering in his black eyes. His gaze settled back on the line of brandy between her legs. He sucked in a breath and held it as he wet his bottom lip and leaned forward to drink it from her body.

His tongue followed the path from her breasts to her pelvis, the duel assault from the cold liquid to his hot tongue affecting her in the most sinful ways. He continued the downward path, until the soft blade of his tongue brushed over her clit. Her fingers gripped the silk scarves holding her down as she throbbed with a renewed excitement. She kept her eyes open, watching his head move as he worked his tongue over her sex.

A storm raged inside her, making her feel ravenous, carnal, completely out of control. He increased the pressure, his tongue lapping harder as he put a finger inside her. Oh God. He pumped, his deft finger brushing over the sensitive bundle inside as heat licked through her blood. She swallowed a whimper, her mind swirling, focused only on the pleasure he was offering.

"Do you want to come for me?" he asked, looking at her from between her legs. "Please answer."

"Yes," she cried out, teetering on the edge of ecstasy as her pussy muscles gripped his finger hard.

"Then you may."

With that, he turned his focus back to her clit, and the second his mouth took possession, her body crumbled into a million tiny pieces. Her nipples throbbed as lust exploded inside her. She panted, growing slicker as she gave herself over to the pleasure. Her body fairly vibrated as her warm cream lubricated his finger, and from deep between her legs she heard Quinn growl.

He stroked deeper, drawing out her pleasure, and when she finally came back down to earth he climbed up her body. His eyes flared hot as they briefly met hers. "I want you on your knees," he murmured into her ear. Looking wild, almost feral, he reached over her head and unleashed her hands, then, none too gently, gripped her hips and flipped her over. Her hair fell across the sheets as he slapped her ass. "Up."

She positioned herself on her hands and knees and felt his cock probe her opening as he gripped her hips hard enough to leave bruises. His fingers bit into her flesh and in one quick thrust he drove into her, stealing the breath from her lungs. She gasped, desperate to refill them, as he pumped deep, the depth of penetration instantly taking her to the edge again.

Controlling the pace and rhythm, Quinn slammed against her, his pelvis crashing against her ass. One hand left her hip, and he slapped her backside, making her yelp in both excitement and pain.

"Silence." He slapped her again.

Desire thrummed through her veins as her pulse leapt. Once again pressure brewed in the depths of her womb, and a whimper bubbled in her throat as it became almost too much to bear. She knew Quinn hadn't heard her sounds over his own grunts.

Her knees quivered and she feared she was going to collapse. As though in tune with her needs, he slipped an arm around her waist and held her upright. His hand splayed over her back as he drove balls deep, and the second she reached her peak, tumbling into another orgasm, he let loose a groan and stilled. She squeezed her pussy, urging him on. His deep growl reverberated through her as he released. His pleasure resonated through her as he jettisoned his seed high inside.

"Fuck," he murmured as he fell over her back once his cock stopped throbbing. His breath was hot on her skin as he worked to regulate his breathing. He stayed still for a moment, then, taking her by surprise, he pulled out and gripped her ankles. He gave a small tug and she dropped to the mattress, the bedding rough against her sensitive nipples.

He slid beside her and ran his fingers through her hair. She turned to him. Even though they'd just had sex, there was restlessness about him as his gaze zeroed in on hers. He flipped her over onto her back and reached between her legs. He cupped her sex, his fingers warm and strong as they held her, making her hyperaware of his strength and power.

His eyes turned a lethal shade of black, and there was a seriousness in his voice when he said, "Mine."

She softened beneath him. "Yours," she whispered without thinking, and as soon as the words left her mouth, she could feel his edginess ebbing away. As exhaustion eased itself into her bones, he pulled her to him, his arms circling her as he cradled her against his shoulder. His hands crushed in her hair and when she stole a glance at him, catching the way the muscles in his jaw relaxed as he gave way to sleep, she felt a new closeness between them.

Her guard slipped and once again she found herself feeling things she swore not to. Quinn was getting under her skin without even trying. This was a game they were playing, she reminded herself, and in this new, unknown world of BDSM she really wasn't sure what was real and what wasn't. Her thoughts shifted, remembering the way he looked at her, the way he made her feel like she was the most-important, most-beautiful woman in the world.

I enjoy being surrounded by beautiful things.

His words came back to haunt her, her mouth going dry as her bliss disappeared. Perhaps he'd spoken them as a way of reminding her that she was just another one of his beautiful things, and nothing other than the sex between them was real. With that last thought in mind, she quickly swallowed down the unwanted emotions working to break through the wall she'd built to protect herself.

This is just sex, Rebecca. Eventually everyone leaves, and you'd be wise to remember that.

Four

Quinn landed his plane on the island's small runaway, keeping his focus on steering them to safety as Rebecca shifted restlessly beside him. Earlier that morning, upon waking in his bed, he had felt a new tension about her. He had chalked up her unease to the things she was going to see and experience at Freedom, the sex resort she'd never made it to last weekend.

The ground crew directed Quinn in and he parked the small Cessna on the tarmac outside the small airport that catered to private aircrafts. You wouldn't find any jumbo jets landing here. Those who came to Freedom had to charter a plane because the island wasn't on the route or radar of any major airline.

He unleashed his harness and turned to her. When he saw her nails digging into her seat, he touched her hand. The flight might have been a bit bumpy due to a front moving in, but he suspected her nervousness stemmed from something else. "Rebecca."

"Yes."

"Relax. Tonight is about watching and learning. Nothing else. Take it in and enjoy the experience. Remember, this is all part of the training period." He reached over and released her seatbelt. "You will be at my side all night and I do believe you *will* take enjoyment in what you're about to experience."

She gave him a wobbly smile, but at least the worry in her eyes had changed to something else, something that looked like intrigue. He opened his door, circled the plane and helped her from her seat. He gathered their luggage and they walked to the front of the airport, where a car awaited them.

They climbed into the car and Rebecca looked around, taking in the other guests milling about—no one rushed on Freedom—and the lush landscape as the driver took them to the posh resort.

He paid the driver and escorted Rebecca up a flower-fringed walkway, leading her inside the lobby of the resort. She kept close to his side, and he could almost hear that brilliant mind of hers working as she took in the rich décor, the couples chatting as they sipped fruity drinks in the airy lobby. A fountain sat in the middle, the sound of water rushing drawing her attention.

"Rebecca," he said, pulling her focus.

She turned to him, and he bit back a grin at her wide-eyed expression. "I'm sorry…what?"

"Do you have any electronics?"

She gave him a perplexed look. "I…have my cell phone."

He held his hand out. "We need to check it." When she frowned, he went on to explain, "No outside electronics or cameras allowed. What happens on Freedom, stays on Freedom."

"Oh," she said, handing it over.

"Come on, let's get you settled in our bungalow."

They hopped on a trolley that would take them to their cabana as the driver put their luggage in the back.

"This place is magnificent," she said as the trolley took them on a tour around the island.

"Are you sorry you missed out last weekend?"

A flush rushed up her neck. "Not at all."

"Good."

The trolley stopped outside his bungalow overlooking the water. Quinn helped Rebecca off as the driver gathered their luggage, opened the door for them, and placed their suitcases in the bedroom. The second Rebecca stepped inside her eyes widened.

"This is beautiful." She spun around, looking at the beachside décor, the one bedroom with a king-sized bed, and the full kitchen he often cooked in when he decided to stay in and relax.

Quinn walked to the fridge and pulled the door open, making sure it was fully stocked as he'd requested. He grabbed two bottles of water and handed one to Rebecca.

"Do you have a standing reservation?" she asked.

"I own it." He took a long pull of the water and put his arm around her waist, turning her toward the ocean. "You are free to come here and use it anytime you like." As soon as the words left his mouth, he visualized Rebecca there without him. Possessiveness rose sure and swift and he instantly squashed it. What the hell was going on with him? Jealousy was foreign to him, and such feelings were reserved for couples. A relationship outside of the lifestyle was out of the question, so he pushed those emotions to the dark recesses of his brain and finished his water.

Late afternoon was upon them and he needed to make an appearance at the dungeon to ensure the stage was set for tonight. "Why don't you have a rest, then explore the island. I have some duties I need to attend to, then I'll be back to collect you for dinner." He glanced at his watch. "How about we meet back here at seven?"

Her smile beamed bright as she looked up at him. "Okay."

She darted into the bedroom to get changed, and Quinn left the bungalow to make his way to the secluded castle in the middle of the resort. He fished his key from his pocket and unlocked the door. Only the most disciplined masters had their own keys. Then again, there was Felix Coffrey. He had one only because his father, renowned billionaire Alexander Coffrey, owned the place. He stepped inside the dark interior and the cool air conditioning fell over him. A noise sounded to his left and he turned.

"Quinn, you're here early."

He squinted, waiting for his eyes to adjust to the dimness, then, when Jacob, the man who oversaw the dungeon, came from the shadows, Quinn held his hand out. "Jacob," he said as they exchanged a handshake. "How are you?"

"Just fine. And you?"

"Excellent." Getting down to business he asked, "Are things in place for tonight?"

"You bet." He led Quinn through the castle to the office at the other end. He pointed to the plush chair behind the desk. "Have a seat."

Quinn sat, and Jacob dropped into the chair opposite him. Jacob nodded to the stack of papers. "I was just pulling the paperwork for our list of attendees for tonight."

"This is everyone?" Quinn looked over the names, revisiting their hard and soft limits and searched for any out-of-place edits." His glance stopped on Felix's paperwork, disappointed that he'd be participating tonight. Then again, why wouldn't he be? As the son of the owner, Felix was a regular fixture in the place. But he was young and cocky and, as far as Quinn was concerned, lacked discipline. Quinn made a mental note to keep an eye on him tonight.

"So far, yes, and I think everyone is familiar to you."

"Great."

"I have do a final check of the rooms and equipment, so I'll let you look that over."

Jacob stood and Quinn said, "Just so you know, I'll have a novice with me tonight."

Jacob angled his head, his eyes narrowing. "You brought someone?"

Since he didn't like the way Jacob was looking at him, he hardened his voice. "If you have a problem with that, voice it now."

"No. I'm just surprised is all. You never—"

Quinn continued to glare at Jacob. Where the hell was all this anger coming from? He liked Jacob, never had a problem with him, and here Quinn was snapping at him for stating the obvious. Yes, it was odd for him to bring a woman to the island, but he'd never met a woman like her, brilliant and beautiful, lacking all pretense. Everything about her was genuine, and damned if it didn't tug at his heart when she looked to him for guidance…reassurance. He took a breath to regroup before speaking.

"She'll wear a white bracelet." No need to explain to Jacob that white meant she'd be observing only.

Jacob nodded toward the locked cabinet, his tone cool when he spoke. "You know where they are."

With that Jacob left and Quinn turned his attention to the paperwork.

Hours later, after Quinn had studied the list of attendees and completed a safety check on the equipment, he made his way back to the bungalow to find Rebecca lounging on a chair outside on the deck. His heart picked up pace as he stood there watching her, and for a minute his thoughts drifted, wondering what it would be like coming home every night to someone like her.

"Hey, you," she said, her eyes opening. "You're in my sun."

"It's almost gone anyway." He gestured to the horizon.

"Time for dinner?"

While he'd like nothing better than to toss her on his bed and spend the rest of the night buried inside her, he nodded. There'd be plenty of time for that later. Right now they needed nourishment, and he wanted to get to the club early to show her around before members started arriving.

He held his hand out to her and pulled her to him. Her warm body collided with his and he slipped his hand around her neck. She wet her lips and he groaned as his mouth crashed down on hers. Jesus, she tasted like candy and honey and spun sugar. In fact, she tasted like forever.

Jerking backward, he broke the kiss and she gave him a quizzical look. "Everything okay?"

Blindsided by the things she made him feel, he let go of her and stepped back, cracking his knuckles to disguise his emotions. "Fine. I just need a shower before we go."

"Okay, I need to get changed anyway."

An hour and a half later, Quinn sat across from Rebecca at the outdoor pavilion. The smile on her face as she enjoyed an after-dinner brandy warmed the darkest corners of his heart. Behind her, he took pleasure in the streaks of orange and purple bruising the summer sky. He shook his head. Honestly, he couldn't remember a time he'd stopped to enjoy the sunset. Then again, he'd been doing a lot of odd things since meeting Rebecca.

"What?" she asked over the rim of her cup.

"You're beautiful," he said.

She blushed. "Thank you. You're not so bad yourself."

He looked at his watch and didn't miss her quick intake of breath.

"Is it time?" she asked in a breathless whisper.

He dropped his napkin, pushed from his chair and reached for her hand. "It's time."

He could practically feel her body vibrating as they walked along the path leading to the dungeon. When she saw the castle's tall spires rising above the trees, she laced her fingers through his. He turned to her and gave a reassuring squeeze. The way she trusted him, reached out for assurance, made him want to shackle her to the St. Andrew's Cross and lose himself in her.

He cleared his throat. "You have nothing to worry about."

"I'm not worried," she answered, then sucked in a breath when the castle came into view. "It's beautiful."

"Not what you expected?"

"No."

Loving that she was pleasantly surprised, he pushed open the front door and they stepped in. She blinked against the dimness as they made their way to the office. Inside, he opened the locked cabinet and fitted her with a bracelet. She held her arm out, examining it.

"What comes after white?"

"Normally blue."

"Normally?"

"Yes. Blue indicates you're a submissive and ready to play," he explained, cringing inside at the thought of her being with another Dom. She opened her mouth, but he cut her off. "Let me show you around before anyone gets here."

He put his hand on the small of her back and guided her down the hall, stopping at each room to let her glance inside.

"Why do only a couple rooms have doors?"

"For safety. Only those fully experienced Doms are allowed to enter a scene behind closed doors." Once again his thoughts raced to Felix, and unease moved through him. He knew the man liked to push his sub's limits, and while Quinn did as well—within reason—Quinn's main concern was his sub's pleasure, not his own. After seeing Felix in action, it was clear he was a cruel Dom, out for his own pleasure.

He took her into a room where the props were stored. "Have a look around." He waved his hand to the wall that held the whips, floggers and canes.

He kept a close eye on her body language as she took in each piece of equipment. She quickly passed over the blindfolds but stopped to touch a few paddles, lingering a moment longer on the one with holes in it. The one she picked up to examine held quite a punch. With the air able to travel through it as he swung, a sub would need a high threshold of pain before they reached subspace.

He showed her a few more rooms and watched the way she stared at the St.

Andrew's Cross in the middle of the room in speechless fascination.

She touched it lightly. "This is…interesting," she said, and as he envisioned her secured to it, his cock throbbed with renewed excitement. He stepped up to her and placed her back against it. Her legs automatically widened and she put her hands above her head.

"How does it feel?" he asked.

Her chest rose and fell erratically, giving him the answer he wanted. Perhaps later, after he was finished with his duties, he'd introduce her to the pleasures of the cross. He quickly dismissed that thought. Tonight was about learning, not participating.

She arched into it. "I think it fits perfectly."

He grinned. "Almost like it was made for you."

"I think it might have been."

"Oh?"

"Well, it is a St. *Andrew's* Cross, and my last name is *Andrews*."

He chuckled. "I hadn't thought of that."

"Quinn?"

"Yeah."

Her lashes blinked rapidly as she stepped away from the cross. "I think I'm ready to fill out my contract."

He smiled just as the castle's bells chimed—an indication that playtime was about to begin. "Okay, but first I'd like for you to invest a few hours into watching some scenes."

She nodded and they made their way to the front of the castle. Quinn greeted each guest as they arrived. He kept a close eye on Rebecca, studying her reactions as a few costumed couples entered the premises. Once everyone had arrived, he shut and locked the heavy front door, then took her hand in his. He brought her to the office again and handed her a bottle of water. She'd been swallowing an awful lot and she looked like she needed it. But now, as he watched her tip her head, exposing the long column of her neck, all he wanted to do was put his mouth there and kiss her sensitive spot until she cried for more.

Clearing his throat, he looked at his watch. Now was not the time to be envisioning her naked and at his mercy. Not when he had duties to attend to. Cursing his cock for not behaving, he said, "All set?"

"So you just make rounds, to make sure everything is okay?"

"That's right."

She recapped her water and left it on the desk. "Then I'm ready."

He stepped up to her and pushed her hair from her face. Leaning into her, he dropped a soft kiss onto her forehead. "I think you're far more ready than you know."

Trailing his hands from her face, down her arms, he captured her hand in his and they moved toward the door. A cacophony of sexy noises reached their ears, and he didn't miss Rebecca's quick intake of breath. He guided her from room to room, exchanging nods with the Doms and subs in play. When Rebecca saw the hot wax play, her eyes lit with intrigue.

She visibly quaked but he could tell it wasn't from fear. She leaned into him. "I thought that would be a hard limit for me. Now I'm not so sure."

His cock swelled. Damn, he loved her openness. How he'd make it through the night without taking her six ways to Sunday was beyond him. "We can try it. If you decide you don't like it, you always have your safe word."

Over the next hour, Quinn continued to introduce her to many different scenes, explaining the process and answering her questions as he monitored the dungeon and its players. When he met with a closed door, his gut tightened. He wasn't a fan of the closed-door policy himself, but some preferred it so he had to respect that.

"Are you allowed to go in?" she whispered.

"It's my duty." Quinn eased the door open quietly and stepped into the room. The scent hit him first. An unpleasant mix of sweat and the clawing fragrance of masculine cologne assailed his nostrils. Then he heard the whimpers. Restrained facedown on a bench, the sub recited her safe word, over and over, only to be ignored by the Dom using a hard cane on her backside. Rage erupted inside Quinn.

"Stop!" Quinn flew across the room, grabbing Felix's arm before he could land another blow on the exhausted female.

Looking somewhat dazed, Felix stared at the hand gripping his wrist, but Quinn suspected he was looking through him not at him. Standing eye-to-eye with the man, who was as tall and broad as Quinn, Quinn snapped his fingers. "Felix," he bit out harshly.

Quinn shot a look over his shoulder, and he spotted Rebecca at the door. She stood deathly still, her mouth open and her eyes wide in terror. He cursed. He grabbed the cane from Felix, resisting the urge to beat the living hell out of him with it and rushed to her.

"Rebecca, kitten, are you okay?"

"I…I think so."

He held her tight and pressed an intercom button near the door. "Jacob, I'm in room three. I need you to come collect Rebecca."

"I'm on my way."

Within seconds Jacob was there, and Quinn released her to him. "Take her to the office. Stay with her."

Looking horrified, Rebecca met his eyes, seeking reassurance. He touched her face, rubbing his thumb over her cheek. "I'll be right there, but I have to take care of this first."

She nodded, and once she disappeared he turned his attention to Felix. Anger rose in him. He crossed the room, unleashed the sub's hands, and helped her to stand. He looked her over and found her trembling and injured. "Are you okay?"

She nodded but his experiences told him she wasn't. He looked at Felix. "You wait here."

He guided the girl to a room where aftercare took place and knew he'd find Sasha inside. Tonight was Sasha's night to monitor the aftercare room. Sasha took one look at the sub and reached for her. He mouthed the word "Felix" and she frowned in understanding. She wrapped the girl in a soft, warm blanket and brought her to the sofa. Knowing the traumatized sub was in good hands, Quinn hurried back to Felix.

He took a few deep breaths, then stepped inside the room, closing the door behind him. "While I would like to show you to the door and never let you return, I can't very well do that."

Felix grinned and ran his hand through short hair cut to the same style as Quinn's. "Daddy wouldn't be pleased."

"Nor would he be pleased at what I just witnessed."

He shrugged. "She was fine."

"You ignored her safe word."

"I couldn't hear it."

Quinn shook his head. "Since you can't master another until you learn to master yourself, you'll be assigned a mentor."

"Come on, Quinn. I don't need a mentor. This is fucking bullshit."

"You do, and you will have one." Quinn turned on the balls of his feet and made for the door. "Follow me to the office. I'll be fitting you with a new bracelet."

"No."

Quinn swung around. The petulant refusal grated on his precariously frayed patience like sandpaper scraping over his teeth. It took two long strides to bring him nose-to-nose with the obnoxious little asshole.

"Obviously that college degree your father bought you by funding the college's new IT department didn't cover a class in common sense, so let me explain how this works…"

Outrage flared in Felix's eyes. "You can't talk to me like that. My daddy…"

"Owns this place."

"That's right." Felix's chin came up.

"And it's one of his most profitable enterprises. It remains a big money maker because it holds an exemplary reputation for adhering to protocols." Quinn tipped his head when Felix broke eye contact. "What? Too many big words? Let me simplify it for you. Your father entrusts the integrity of his businesses to people who make the right decisions. Tonight, that person is me. This shit you pulled? Not the first time it's happened, and your daddy knows it." The look on Felix's face was priceless. "That's right. He gets biweekly reports on everything, including disciplinary action taken on both members and staff. This is your third offense. One more and you're out of here."

"You're a dick."

"And you're a sadistic little prick with no integrity whatsoever. If you want to continue your membership here, you'll play by the rules or you'll walk." Quinn stepped out of Felix's personal space and indicated the open door, biting back a satisfied grin when the other man suddenly realized that anyone passing by had been privy to his dressing down. "After you."

Felix glared at Quinn, and, acting like a petulant child, he kicked the bench his sub had occupied across the floor before preceding Quinn down the long hall leading to the office.

Inside, Quinn found Rebecca sitting at the desk across from Jacob. She glanced up, her gaze moving between him and Felix. She hadn't run. Relief slammed into his chest like a cannon ball. She sat perched on a chair, a pen poised over a small stack of papers. He didn't want Felix anywhere near his girl and hated that she'd witnessed his ignorance in a scene, but he needed to bring him to the office to replace his band.

Felix's surly expression immediately transformed when he saw Rebecca. He shot her his trademark playboy smile, flashing dimples and several thousands of dollars' worth of orthodontic work, and ran his hand through his hair. Ignoring Quinn's warning glare, he stepped forward, glancing at the contract she had been filling out. Quinn shot Jacob a questioning glance.

"She didn't have one on file so I thought…" Jacob let his words fall off and looked away.

Quinn swore under his breath. Now was not the time for Rebecca to go over her limits, especially after having witnessed Felix cross a line with his sub. Since it was too late to do anything about it at this point, Quinn huffed out an exasperated breath and purposefully stepped between her and Felix as the man put out his hand for a shake, effectively stopping him from touching Rebecca.

"Back up," Quinn said, and when Felix put a measure of distance between him and Rebecca, Quinn went to the locked cabinet behind the desk. He unlocked it, grabbed a braided yellow leather bracelet and handed it to Felix. Felix reluctantly took his off and put the new one on.

"You're out of here for the rest of the night." Quinn pressed a button under his desk. "I'll have security walk you out."

"You're ordering me around? In an establishment that my daddy owns?"

"I'm in charge here. Don't ever forget that," Quinn bit out. He drew a breath to get his temper in check before he personally removed the smirk from the spoiled little prick's face.

Felix hardened at his words. The smile fell, and rage move in to take its place. "We'll see about that."

Two security guards walked in and Quinn handed Felix over.

The second he was gone, he turned to Rebecca and touched her face. "I'm sorry you had to witness that."

"What does the yellow bracelet mean?" she asked.

"It means he's in yield position." He pulled her from the chair. "He'll be assigned a mentor."

"A mentor?"

He sat and pulled her on to his lap. "He needs to learn discipline. Believe me, we don't tolerate that kind of behavior here."

"Then you should be his mentor."

"Fuck. No."

"I think he should learn from the best."

Her confidence in him filled him with pride and he felt a curious shift inside him. There was no question that in a short amount of time she'd taken up residency in his heart and had him considering something he'd never, ever considered before—collaring her and expressing his devotion, his level of commitment to her. That thought frightened him almost as much as it excited him. Sure, he had cheating blood running through his veins. But Rebecca made him want to try to break the pattern. Made him want to be a better man, the only man—for her.

"Is his…is the girl okay?"

Feeling a little off his game at that revelation, he checked his watch. "She will be."

"Do you need to go?"

"It'll soon be closing time, and I need to do another check."

She slid from his lap and moved to the door, a sexy sway to her hip. She moved toward the door. "I'll come with you." His gaze dropped to a lush backside that he couldn't wait to cradle in his hands. She turned to him and his eyes moved to her soft, round breasts hidden beneath her blouse.

He stood and looked at the contract, noticing the big X by blindfolds, but other than that she now seemed open to trying many things. He filed her papers, deciding to go over them tomorrow when she had more time to digest tonight's events. He turned to her, and his heart pounded a little bit harder as he took in the excitement, the curiosity in her eyes. He fisted his hands to occupy them, resisting the temptation to rip off her clothes and ravish her right there in the office. His cock swelled as visions of the two of them coming together filled his thoughts, and he couldn't help but think maybe he'd start her training sooner rather than later.

Five

A fine shiver moved through Rebecca, stopping at every erogenous zone along the way as she watched Quinn lead the last of the players out of the castle. The lock clicked into place and when he turned to her, the heat in his eyes, the way he looked at her, made her want to drop to her knees in submission.

Outside of the Felix incident, tonight's events had raised her curiosity. She was anxious to be tied up and taken by the powerful Dom who was currently looking at her like he wanted to eat her alive. He'd said she wasn't ready to play, but deep in her heart, she knew she'd been ready for a very long time now. In an effort to show him just how much she wanted this, just how ready she really was, she sank to her knees and lowered her head.

"Rebecca," he groaned. She knew he wasn't a man who rattled easily, and it excited her to know she had the ability to fluster him.

"Yes?" she asked, lifting her eyes slightly. He was tense, like he was fighting an internal battle. He stood motionless, save for the clenching and unclenching of his fingers. When she didn't think she could stand another moment waiting, he reached down, slipped his hand around her neck, and grabbed a fistful of her hair. He tugged until her eyes met his.

"Yes who?"

Her pulse leapt as he stepped into the role of her master. "Yes, sir," she answered, realizing that they were now in high protocol.

His voice changed, hardened as he tugged her hair with a little more force. "On your feet."

She stood, and as his heat and passion reached out to her, she lowered her eyes, getting into the right headspace for what was to come.

"Are you trying to tempt me again, like you did at your office?" he asked. "Answer, please."

She stole a peek at him, and knew her eyes were full of want as they met his. "Yes, sir," she said honestly, her whole body trembling.

He shook his head, the muscles along his jaw ticking. "Once again I find you trying to take control from me." She remained quiet, waiting, hoping for more. "I won't tolerate this kind of behavior, kitten."

Electricity sizzled between them. "Sorry, sir."

"I believe it's time for me to take you over my knee… Or better yet…"

His words trailed off as he took her hand in his and hurried her through the castle, moving like a man who knew what he wanted and knew how to get it. When he ushered her into the room with the cross, she was pretty sure she'd died and gone to heaven. Her chest heaved but she worked to keep herself from showing too much excitement.

His eyes held hers. "Tell me your safe word."

"Freedom."

"Say it again."

"Freedom."

"Undress," he commanded.

With shaky fingers, she removed her blouse and skirt, standing before him in nothing but her black bra and thong.

His eyes went dark as they dropped to her hips. "Did we not already have the talk about panties?"

"I didn't know." She drew in air and let it out quick. "You said I wouldn't be playing tonight."

He stepped up to her and in one deft movement he unclasped her bra. As it fell to the floor, he gripped the lace on her panties and gave a quick tug, ripping the slip of material from her hips.

"Any time you're with me," he reminded her. "You do want to please me, don't you?"

"Yes."

"Then why do you continue to defy me?"

"It won't happen again…sir."

"It had better not." He put his mouth close to her ear. "Otherwise, I'll put you over my knee, and I won't be so gentle."

"Oh," she said, her voice a breathless whisper.

He backed her up until she was pressed against the cross, his lips still by her ear. "Turn around," he commanded, the rush of air from his mouth brushing over her naked flesh.

She obliged, facing the cross, and in her next breath he shackled her hands and legs. With her now at his mercy, his palms roamed her body, exploring her every curve, her every crevice.

He leaned into her and his scent fell over her like a powerful aphrodisiac. His hard cock dug into her back and her nipples tightened painfully. Her body hummed with excitement. She drew in a breath and held it, certain she'd never been more aroused in her life.

Suddenly, he was gone, leaving her in the room all alone, completely naked and secured to a cross. A shiver stole over her as anticipation raced through her veins, the wait for his return, for him to touch her, nearly killing her.

The sound of footsteps heralded his approach and her breath came a little quicker when she felt his mouth near her ear. "I believe my kitten needs to learn a thing or two." He walked around the cross and heat bombarded her when she saw the paddle in his hand. This one lacked the air holes and she guessed he wanted to introduce her to pain slowly—in the heat of the moment she was thankful that he was such a caring Dom. He spun the piece of equipment in his hands, his eyes going to hers, gauging her reactions.

He looked her over for a moment, then said, "Eyes down."

She tore her glance away as he circled her again, his drawn-out foreplay building the eagerness inside her. He stilled behind her and she felt his hand on her backside. He grazed his fingers over her skin, traced the shape of her curves so lightly that her flesh quivered for more when he stopped. The next touch came from the paddle. She gasped at that first sweet whack, and her body banged against the cross.

His hand moved over her ass, soothing the burning sting before the paddle hit again. Oh God, it felt so erotic, stimulating. Hot. The third whack brought a blistering heat that exploded inside her, and she gave herself over to the pain and pleasure, letting it take her to a place she'd never been before.

As she basked in her sexual awakening, her head fell forward, wanting, needing…something…but not exactly sure what that something was. The paddle came across her cheeks again, then he used his hand to soothe the sting, creating a need inside her unlike anything she'd experienced in the past. Her sex muscles clenched, eager for something to grip. Her brain shut down, focusing only on the pleasure racing through her.

His voice was low, hard when he asked, "Are you going to try to take control again?" He waited a moment, then said, "Answer, please."

"No, sir," she breathed out, ever determined to please him.

"Very well."

His hands went to her shackles and he freed her, then turned her. He pressed her back against the cross as she faced him. Her arms fell to her sides. She let out a shuddering breath, her body trembling with need. She waited for his instructions, but when none came, she read the command in his eyes and lifted her hands.

"That's a good girl." He shackled her again and touched her mouth, running his thumb over her lips. He leaned in and kissed her with such passion it left her gulping for her next breath. His mouth moved to her breasts. His tongue felt like fire on her skin, and she arched into him. He pushed her back, until she was flat against the cross, her body pinned beneath his hands. She listened to his breath as he sank lower, pressing his nose to her skin.

She wanted to move, to cry, to writhe, as heat flooded her. His hand dipped between her open legs. "If I touch you, will I find you wet for me?" His gaze drilled into hers. "Answer, please."

"Yes, sir."

He moved his fingers higher, until he touched her outer lips. She bit back a cry of pleasure, wanting to jerk forward, to force him inside. He pulled her lips open, then dipped a finger into her heat.

"My, my," he said. His finger brushed over her clit, so soft, so feather light. "My kitten is so needy."

This time she didn't care about the punishment, she just wanted, needed…that something again. "Please," she murmured as her body called out to him, pleading for his touch.

"Hush," he warned, and none too gently, he pinched her clit. Pleasure resonated through her and she swallowed a whimper. He pushed a finger into her. "Is this what you need?"

Since he hadn't yet told her to speak, she clamped her mouth shut, concentrating on the way he was stroking the sensitive bundle of nerves inside her. When she liquefied under his touch, he bit out, "Don't you dare come."

She tried to press her thighs together, to keep his fingers inside her, but the clamps held her legs apart. A cry lodged in her throat. It was erotic, stimulating, blissful torture.

"I'm not sure I'll even let you come," he said. "I like seeing you like this."

Oh God!

He went down on his knees and leaned into her, tasting between her legs. The heat of his fingers was nothing compared to his tongue. It seared her, making her feel wild, out of control, so damn insane. Unrelenting pressure brewed in the depths of her womb and her pussy quaked as he ravaged her.

"Move your hips, kitten. Fuck my tongue."

Good God!

She rocked against him, wanting to drive her pussy into his face, but he pulled back, offering her the tip of his tongue only. Her hips jerked forward, her clit catching the blade of his tongue with each thrust. Even though it was light, the impact took her higher and higher. It surprised her really, but it shouldn't have. Quinn's skills, and his ability to read her body, knew no limits.

Her body burned from the inside out, and as her clit swelled she wasn't sure how long she could hold on. She pulled against the straps holding her arms, wanting to grab his head and force his mouth to her quivering pussy.

Moisture broke out on her skin, and her hair fell forward as her blood ignited to a near boil.

"Look at you, kitten." The second his finger replaced his tongue on her clit, she knew she was done for. He must have known it too, because he said, "You may come."

Her entire body exploded, her orgasm so powerful her mind completely shut down. As the waves took hold, she rode them out, savoring each and every rise and fall. She sucked in a breath, working to refill her lungs, but the next thing she knew Quinn was shedding his clothes. His beautiful cock reached out to her and she whimpered.

His hands went to hers and he held them as he positioned his cock between her legs. Her eyes met his, and honest to God, she never seen him so intense before. His nostrils flared as one hand fell to her waist. His arms circled around her back and he gripped her hard as he drove into her so fast and so deep that there was nothing she could do to keep a cry at bay.

Sexual energy swirled around them, racing over her body and exploding her senses. His cock filled her, and as his low moan fell over her, she knew he was close to losing it. Her addled brain swirled, basic elemental need taking over. A shudder moved through her as he pulled almost all the way out, only to slam back inside again.

Feeling desperate to keep him inside, she squeezed her muscles, and he groaned.

"Cut it out," he growled.

He pounded his pelvis against her clit, and an orgasm hit, taking her by complete surprise.

"Fuck," he bit out as her liquid heat soaked his cock and dripped down her thighs.

Her nipples scraped over his chest and she could feel his heart pounding against his ribcage. With his chest pressed against hers, he threw his head back and came with a growl. His cock pulsed hard inside her as he depleted himself. She sucked in a breath, happy to be secured, otherwise she was sure she would have fallen to her knees.

He buried his mouth in the crook of her neck, his breath hot on her skin as he panted and struggled for air. Their bodies shook, her chest rose and fell erratically, and when he inched back to pull out, he cupped her face and planted a soft kiss on her mouth. She kissed him back, loving the taste of him on her tongue and never wanting the moment to end. He broke the kiss and unleashed her wrists, and with gentle, caring hands, he rubbed the slight red marks on her skin.

She looked into his eyes and her heart hitched. She had expected a skilled Dominant, but what she hadn't expected was his underlying tenderness. He bent and released her legs, then gathered her in his arms. Feeling a little unstable, she sank into his comfort and rested her head against his. He found a blanket, draped it over her, then carried her back to his cabana. He placed her on the bed and crawled in beside her. Warm hands held her tight and it generated warmth and need inside her. He stroked her hair, the intimacy in the way he was touching her taking her breath away.

Sleep pulled at her, and as she began to drift off it occurred to her that she hadn't felt this kind of connection in a long time.

Correction… In forever.

Six

Rebecca awoke to the sound of the surf lapping against the sandy shore. She blinked and stretched, her sore muscles reminding her of her incredible night with Quinn.

Quinn.

He touched her on a level she'd never experienced before, took her to heights of sexual satisfaction that left her completely sated. That he could do this in the short time they'd been together was a bit frightening.

She reached across the bed, but when she found it empty she jackknifed upward. She looked around the bedroom, searching for some indication as to where he'd gone. Her eyes settled on the clock and she was surprised to see it was nearly noon. Her body must have really needed the rest; she couldn't remember the last time she'd slept so late.

Stretching, she kicked off her blankets and threw her legs over the side of the bed. She was still naked. She looked for her phone to see if he'd texted but then remembered she'd had to turn it in at check-in. The smell of coffee wafted before her nose and she smiled, expecting to find Quinn in the kitchen. She padded down the hall and found a note on the counter.

You looked so peaceful sleeping I didn't want to wake you. Sorry I wasn't there when you woke, but I had some business to take care of. Be sure to eat breakfast, I have something special planned and you're going to need your strength.

She reread the letter before she put it back down, a huge smile on her face. Wondering what he was up to, she made herself a cup of coffee and sipped it on the way to the shower. She stayed under the spray, lingering longer than normal. She basked in the hot water, let it soothe her soreness. She couldn't remember the last time she'd had an unhurried morning. The water turned cold and she climbed out, towel dried her body and ran a comb through her hair. She looked at herself in the mirror and hardly recognized the sated woman staring back.

She pulled on a sundress, her favorite Via Spiga open-toe sandals and nothing else, remembering Quinn's instructions. After refilling her coffee, she stepped outside, anxious for Quinn to return. It was crazy how much she wanted to see him, how much she missed his presence, his touch. She lowered herself into a chaise lounge and tipped her face to the sun, closing her eyes against the brightness and enjoying the heat of the noonday warmth.

A few moments later, a shadow fell over her. She smiled and stretched lazily.

"Quinn…"

"Sorry."

"Oh," Rebecca bolted upright at the unfamiliar voice. She brought her hand up, shielding her eyes as they adjusted to the sun. "Felix?"

"That's right."

Frowning, she tipped her head. "What are you doing here?"

Shoving his hands in his pockets, Felix glanced down the walkway leading from the bungalow. "Quinn asked me to collect you."

Her brow furrowed. Why would Quinn ask Felix to come for her? He didn't even like the man. She couldn't imagine any reason he'd send him for her. Unless… "He's decided to be your mentor?"

An odd, almost relieved expression passed over Felix's face. "Yes, exactly."

She pushed from her chair and stood. "Where is he?"

"He asked me to take you to the castle. He has a surprise for you."

In the note he'd said he had a surprise, but still something felt…off. She wished she could text him to make sure.

Felix winked. "We'd better hurry. His patience only goes so far."

She smiled, relaxing slightly. "You're right about that."

He waved his hand. "Shall we?"

She moved in beside Felix, walking at his side along the flower-fringed walkway leading to the castle. He ran his hand through his hair in a move that reminded her of last night, and once again she felt a moment of hesitation.

But then he smiled, and said, "It's a beautiful day to be on the island, isn't it?"

"It is," she agreed.

"This is your first time here?"

She nodded, not really comfortable divulging too much information to him. Even though he was a Dom under Quinn's care, he was a stranger to her.

When they reached the castle, he pulled a key from his pocket and unlocked the door. Something niggled in the back of her mind as he opened it and ushered her inside. She blinked against the dimness, and when he set the lock behind him, another wave of unease moved through her, her intuition warning that something was wrong. Seriously wrong.

"Is he in the office?" she asked, working to sound casual as her fight-or-flight instincts kicked in.

He nodded. "I believe you know the way."

She quickened her pace, but he was so close behind her she could almost feel his breath on her neck. She reached the office and pushed the door open. "Quinn," she said as she entered. When she found it empty, she spun around to run back out. Felix caught her at the door, knocking her to the floor. She screamed as his knee dug into her back, and when she felt a pair of handcuffs lock her wrists together, she gasped in horror.

"What the hell do you think you're doing?" she asked, pitching her voice low like she'd been taught in self-defense class. Some good that was doing her now.

"Showing Quinn who's really in charge." He pulled her to his feet. "If he's going to fuck with me and my sub, then I'm going to fuck with his."

Her heart pounded as he dragged her down the hall to the room she and Quinn had played in last night. Her brain raced, eager to stop this. She mentally kicked herself for falling for his line of bullshit. She was an intelligent woman, so why she'd ignored her intuition was beyond her.

Because Quinn was involved...

Felix pushed her into the room and backed her up against the cross. He bent to shackle her legs and she drew her foot back and kicked him in the face as hard as she could. He cursed and dropped to the ground, and she ran for the door. She had to get out, and fast. She'd seen the maniacal pleasure he'd taken in beating his sub. He wasn't playing out a scene gone wrong now. He was hell bent on extracting revenge and Quinn wasn't here to come to her rescue.

With her hands locked behind her back, she didn't get very far. Felix's bellow of rage reached her just before he did. He took her down like a linebacker. The doorframe caught her on the temple. Light exploded behind her eyes as he dragged her to the tiled floor. The room spun and her stomach pitched as he struggled to pick her up. She went limp, making it even more difficult for him to maneuver her. Finally, he gathered her in a bear hug, grunting and cursing through lips swollen from the kiss of her wedge sandals. She let him wrestle her around a bit longer and, when he had her in just the right position, threw her head forward, catching him in the nose.

"Stop," he cried out as he shoved her against the cross, her head ricocheting off the bars.

Blood trickled from Felix's nose to his lip. It gave her an enormous amount of satisfaction, but using her head as a weapon amplified her dizziness and the buzzing in her ears from the injury to her temple. So much so that he managed to get the strap around one of her ankles. She kicked at him with her free foot, hoping to get another shot in, but this time he managed to dodge her. When he grabbed her other leg and secured it as well, she knew it was time to change tactics.

"Quinn is going to be here any minute. This morning we made plans to meet here at noon."

"Nice try," he muttered, shoving her head against the cross. "I'm not an idiot. I know exactly where Mr. 'Play by the Rules' Quinn Montgomery is."

He walked behind her and unhooked her hands, holding them tight in one of his big palms. He stepped to the side and drew one hand over her head. She tried to fight with the other but he grabbed it and squeezed hard. The cry of pain came out before she could stop it. He secured it in place, then stepped in front of her. When his gaze slid to hers, the gleam of satisfaction there sent a flash of fear down her spine. "And I know exactly what I'm doing."

"Felix, please don't do this."

"You better shut up, or I'll put a gag in your mouth. Then again you'd probably like it. Considering you didn't mark an X by it on your contract."

Her heart pounded against her ribs. He'd seen her contract? Oh God, when he'd been in the office last night he'd seen her contract! He knew what she liked, but more importantly…what she didn't.

He reached around and pulled a blindfold from his back pocket and when he twirled it around his index finger, a cry caught in her throat. "What's the matter?" With a cruel smile curling up his mouth, he stepped up to her. "Afraid of the dark?"

"Don't!" She shook her head hard. "Please don't. I'll do anything you want."

He gave the blindfold another twirl and then caught it in his fist. Watching her, he ran the shiny fabric between his thumb and forefinger. "What would you do?"

Her nostrils flared with the force of her breathing. "Anything. What do you want?"

His gaze moved over her, head-to-toe and back again. "I want it all," he answered.

"Quinn," she cried out, hysteria rising in her.

"He can't hear you, kitten. No one can hear your cries."

In that moment her mind went back in time, to the frightened girl locked in the basement with no sight, using every ounce of mental strength she had to make it until freedom. Freedom. God! The irony of that word wasn't lost on her as Felix readjusted her shackles, tightening them to the point of pain. She'd long ago sworn she'd never allow herself to be put in such a vulnerable situation again, yet here she was, locked inside her own head with her demons snapping at her heels, helpless while some man was going to take what he wanted from her.

He slipped the blindfold over her forehead. Her scream lodged in the back of her throat, a soundless cry for help that no one would hear, and then the world around her went black.

Yours to Keep

One

With a little extra spring in his step, Quinn Montgomery left the air-conditioned lobby of Freedom, his favorite, members-only resort a few miles off the coast of beautiful Nova Scotia. He walked outside, lifting his face to the sky to enjoy the late-morning sun as he thought about the woman waiting in his bed.

He breathed in the fragrant island smells of lilac, pine and marigolds, and his ears perked at the murmurs and soft, sexy sounds coming from the nearby pool. He glanced around the private resort to take in all the couples in various stages of undress. In the past he'd often joined his friends in such activities, had often tag-teamed with his buddies for a little early-morning entertainment. But now, well…now the only girl he wanted in his life, in his bed—on her knees in front of him—was Rebecca Andrews, the smart and sexy lawyer who'd gotten under his skin without even trying.

He looked off in the distance and let loose a contented sigh. Almost one year ago to the day, that smart mouth of hers had taken him down in the courtroom. His company might have lost a substantial amount of money to her client, but it was worth every penny, because here they were now, with him taking *her* down in the bedroom, and giving her everything she'd ever wanted.

He'd meant to take her training slow, but when she stared at him with curious eyes, how could he not respond to her needs and lead her down a path to sensual freedom sooner rather than later?

Quinn checked his watched and hurried his steps. No doubt she'd be awake and looking for him by now. She'd been sleeping so soundly when he awoke—compliments of a late night at the castle where he'd shackled her wrists and ankles and introduced her to a darker side of pleasure. Instead of waking her, he'd left her a note letting her know he had business to take care of. It wasn't a lie. He did have things to take care of, and while he hated to leave their bed, he wasn't ready for her to know what he was up to. Not yet, anyway.

It was shocking how much he'd changed since she'd first dropped to her knees and called him "sir". For reasons beyond his understanding, he couldn't quite get enough of her, even though he'd sworn off relationships long ago. The Montgomery blood was tainted with cheaters, but for Rebecca he'd do whatever it took to change that pattern.

Quinn wanted to be the man for her—the man she both wanted and needed. That revelation had driven him from their bed and to the lobby, where he called in a favor from his favorite jeweler. If things went according to plan, then soon enough Rebecca would be his, and his only. She'd given him her body, now it was time to break through her mental barriers and show her she had nothing to fear before he held a collaring ceremony and expressed his level of devotion.

He cracked his knuckles in anticipation. When it came to getting what he wanted, he was ruthless in his pursuits. It was that internal drive that had turned him into a successful billionaire at the young age of thirty.

He veered off the main walking path and strolled along the shoreline, his sandals sinking into the warm white sand as he waved to those passing by on their luxury yachts. His mind traveled back to last night, to the way Rebecca had opened herself to him. His cock thickened when he recalled the softness in her voice, to the way she'd so readily surrendered her body.

His breath came quicker and he drew in the salty tang of the ocean, adjusting his erection inside his khaki shorts as he made his way along the sandy shore toward his cabana, anxious to continue with her training. His fingers itched as he thought about that sweet backside of hers and how much he wanted to put her over his knee again.

Up ahead he spotted Jacob, the man who oversaw the BDSM castle. His bare feet crushed the sand beneath him as he jogged along the beach toward Quinn. His advance was rapid, and when his gaze met Quinn's, a puzzled look moved over his face.

Jacob slowed as he approached, then came to a stop. Hands on hips, he took a couple breaths. "Quinn," he greeted.

Quinn was an expert at reading others, and even if he wasn't, from the strange way Jacob was looking at him, it was easy to tell something was wrong. He shaded his eyes and looked past Jacob's shoulder. He searched the beach, scanning for signs of trouble.

He focused in on Jacob. "What is it?"

Jacob's gaze went from Quinn, to the castle's tall spires puncturing the overhead clouds, then back to Quinn again. He raked his fingers through his damp hair. "How did you get here so fast?"

Quinn angled his head and looked over his friend. He arched a brow and grinned. "Have you been jogging in the sun too long?" He jerked his thumb over his shoulder. "I just came from the lobby."

Jacob shot another quick glance toward the castle, "But I...I just saw you with Rebecca."

Quinn looked toward the castle. Jacob had to be mistaken. "Rebecca's at the cabana waiting for me." She had no reason to go to the castle.

Jacob scratched the back of his head. "I'm pretty sure it was her. I'm almost certain."

"Like you were certain it was me?" Quinn laughed, and put his hand on his friend's shoulder. "I think you need to get out of the sun, pal."

"Jesus, I must be losing it." He shook his head. "Either that, or you two both have twins."

"Wait. What?" A flash of unease moved through Quinn and his smile dissolved.

"You both must have twins," he repeated.

Quinn stared down the beach and considered the members on the island who might resemble him enough for Jacob to think Rebecca was with him, then he turned his attention back to Jacob. The man wasn't prone to rash comments, and the confusion on his face was genuine. Quinn had learned early on to trust his gut instincts, and right now it was telling him to listen. Something was wrong.

"Are you sure it was her?" he asked.

"Yeah."

"And she was with someone who resembled me?"

"From the back anyway."

His mind raced, then came to a resounding halt.

Fuck.

Quinn might not have a twin, but there was one man at the resort with the same build and stature, a man he'd stood eye to eye with last night. With single-minded determination, he ran full throttle toward the dungeon. His heart crashed against his chest as he took a direct path that circumvented the winding walkway. He pushed through the bushes, cutting left and right to avoid a collision with the century-old pine trees. He broke through the trees near the castle and darted up the stairs. Shaky hands fished the key from his pocket as fear crept in and squeezed his gut. He pushed through the main door, shoving so hard it banged off the wall, the crash reverberating through the huge, airy castle.

"Rebecca," he called out. He blinked, willing his eyes to adjust to the darkness. He shot a glance around, struggling to see in the dark. When he heard a cry coming from one of the rooms, he rushed down the hall toward it.

The second he saw her—arms and legs shackled to the cross, a blindfold covering her eyes—his heart slid into his throat. Oh, fuck no.

No. No. No.

"Rebecca," he said quickly, protectiveness firing his brain. "Oh Jesus, Rebecca." He started toward her, and from his peripheral vision spotted Felix stepping around the cross. Fury clawed at his insides, demanding he beat the man dead. But at the moment, the need to rip that fucking covering off her face, to free her from the nightmares that came with crossing a hard limit, was far more important than tearing into Felix.

Quinn extended his hand, but seconds before he reached the blindfold, Felix rammed into him from the side, sending him flying across the room. He landed with a thud and air rushed from his lungs. Christ! He climbed to his feet as Felix came toward him again.

Quinn ducked and drove into the man's stomach, tackling him to the ground. They both went down hard, the anger coursing through his body so toxic he could taste it on the tip of his tongue. They rolled, but Quinn gained purchase. He pinned the fucker to the floor, and knew in an instant he was going to kill him, and he was going to enjoy every fucking second of it.

He drove his knees into Felix's chest to hold him down. Quinn's body vibrated at the rush of adrenaline as he fisted his hands and pounded the man's face. A chorus of violent sounds echoed in the room and red bled into the whites of Felix's eyes as he struggled to protect himself. He failed miserably, unable to stop the assault. Too fucking bad. Now he'd know what Rebecca felt like.

As he continued to pummel Felix, the coppery scent of blood filled the air. The tang urged him on, but some small part of his brain registered Rebecca's cries.

Rebecca.

His stomach tightened and he jumped to his feet. He left Felix in a pool of blood and rushed to the woman who'd come to mean so much to him.

"Take it off! Take it off!" she shrieked.

He ripped the blindfold from her eyes, and when his gaze met with terror, he almost sobbed. His heart squeezed to the point of pain.

"Rebecca." He cupped her face, his hands still shaking as he held her. He softened his words, a breathless whisper, when he said, "I'm here, kitten. I'm here."

She tried to pull away. "No, don't," she cried out, her voice rising to the point of hysteria. "Stop, go away. Go away!"

His throat tightened. Jesus Christ, he'd never felt so powerless in his life. He tried to touch her but she struggled against him, chanting something incoherent under her breath.

"Rebecca," he said again.

The chanting continued, and if he wasn't mistaken she was reciting the alphabet. This was bad, so fucking bad. He needed to help but his soft, soothing words weren't enough to break through the nightmare of having been kidnapped and blindfolded. Perhaps his dominant tone might. He hardened his voice.

"Rebecca, I've got you."

She looked at him, unfocused, her mind somewhere else completely. Jesus Christ, where had she gone? Her chest was rising and falling so hard she was going to hyperventilate and pass out. He needed to snap her out of it, and he needed her to do it now.

"Rebecca," he said again, tapping her cheek to bring her back.

She blinked three times, and her gaze darted around the room before turning to him. "What… Where?"

"Rebecca. You're safe. It's me, Quinn."

"Quinn," she said around a sob, her body sagging.

The fear in her voice nearly killed him. His blood ran cold and he clenched his teeth, wanting nothing more than to drag Felix back to standing and beat him again for doing this to her.

His body tensed as he looked at the man struggling to climb to his feet. Blood oozed from his mouth, his nose, and pooled on the floor around him. He went up on his hands and knees, but his palms slid forward and he groaned as he landed with a hard thud on his chest. Fuck him. He wasn't going anywhere soon. Quinn would deal with him after he took care of Rebecca.

A garbled sound caught in Rebecca's throat. Shit, she shouldn't be seeing any of this. Quinn cupped her head, forcing her to focus on him, not the bastard on the floor. He tamped down his anger. That's not what she needed from him right now.

He pressed his forehead to hers, and her tears fell harder. He wiped his hands on his khakis, scrubbing away as much of the blood as he could before he touched her. Thumb under her chin, he gently lifted her face until their eyes met, then brushed away the stream of tears. "Rebecca, sweetheart…" he began, but how could he reassure her that everything was okay when it wasn't? Fuck. Her hard limit had been crossed. She might never come back from that.

She sagged into him and struggled against the bindings. Quinn quickly released her, rubbing the red chafe marks on her skin. Another rush of anger cut through him. The fucker had strapped her too tightly and nearly cut off her circulation. He sucked in a breath and let it out slowly. After he'd seen her to safety, he was going to enjoy coming back here and fucking the bastard over some more.

With her muscles seizing and her joints rebelling, her body was about to collapse. He ran his hands over her arms, gently massaging her muscles and warming her cold, clammy skin, but she began to shake harder. Christ, she was going into shock. He quickly gathered her in his arms and scanned the room for a blanket.

To work against the shock, he hurried to the aftercare room and grabbed a blanket from the electric, stainless steel blanket-warmer cabinet. He swathed her in it and darted outside, nearly crashing into Jacob as he rushed up the castle stairs toward them.

Jacob's eyes widened then he hissed in air. "Felix?"

Quinn nodded. He jerked his head toward the door and lowered his voice. "Get ahold of security, but I want to see him before they take him away. I'm not done with him."

Jacob nodded. "What about his father?"

"Alexander Coffrey might own the castle and half the island, but he's a reasonable man. I'll deal with him later. Right now I need you to send a medic to my cabana." Jacob nodded and Quinn hurried down the stairs, desperate to get Rebecca away from all this.

Quinn ran through the resort, anger seething from every pore in his body. He mentally kicked himself. How could he have let this happen to her? She was so unsure of this world that he'd brought her into, and he'd promised he'd to take care of her, that he'd always ensure her safety. He was a man of his word—he prided himself on that—but he'd let her down. No way could he ever forgive himself for that.

A soft sound caught in her throat, and her body shook, almost violently. He gathered her closer and ran faster, his mind going over the events of last night and what he could have done differently. One thing was for certain. He should have taken Felix's key. Regardless of who his father was, he should have taken the key and had him removed from the island for abusing his sub. A hard lesson learned, and a mistake he wouldn't make with any other Dom who sidestepped the rules.

He reached his cabana and shouldered the door open. Once inside he hurried to the bedroom. He removed the utilitarian blanket and tucked her between the soft Egyptian sheets so she'd have something familiar against her body, then pulled the comforter over her. She blinked rapidly, and he slid in beside her, offering his warmth and security.

"Quinn," she murmured.

He went up on his elbow and pulled her in tighter. "I'm here, Rebecca. I'm here. You're safe."

Fear reflected in her eyes as she pressed a shaky hand to his chest. He closed his palm over hers, giving her a reassuring squeeze as worry clawed at his gut.

"Take me home," she said, jerking her hand back. Shit, she hadn't been touching him for comfort, she'd been pushing him away.

Her rejection stung like a slap in the face, but he fucking deserved it. "The doctor is on his way. You need to be looked at."

She shook her head, the soft brush of her hair on the pillow grating over his heart at her rejection. "No, what I need is for you take me home right now."

"Rebecca…" he began cautiously, then shut his mouth when she shook her head harder.

"I need to be away from all of this." She turned from him, and he couldn't see her face when she curled up in the fetal position and added, "Away from you."

Two

Rebecca closed the file on her desk. She let out a slow breath, stole a glance at her clock and sank back into her chair. The familiar noises outside her office gave her a modicum of comfort, reminding her she was back in Manhattan, safe from Felix…the blindfold. It had been three days since she'd left the private island and while she wanted to forget about Felix, and the darkness that took her back to the fearful days of her childhood, she was having a much harder time putting Quinn out of her thoughts.

Quinn.

He'd been so sweet, incredibly concerned and caring after finding her tied to the cross, and for the first time since they'd met, she'd seen him come undone. She hadn't *seen* him beat Felix half to death, since she had the blindfold on, but she'd heard each curse that had fallen from Quinn's mouth as he pummeled his fists into her captor's face. But after he'd taken if off, she saw the mess of blood on the dungeon floor, saw Felix rolling around in it and moaning in agony. She had no idea what had happened to him after the beating. Her only thought had been to escape, return to the comfort and familiarity of her condo in Manhattan. Quinn had only told her that he would take care of matters, and she wasn't sure she wanted to know any more than that.

A shiver moved through her, and she wrapped her arms around herself as she climbed to her feet and walked to her window. She glanced at the sofa, or more specifically, to the package she'd found waiting for her when she returned to her office Monday morning. It had been delivered to her office complex last Saturday, which meant Quinn must have arranged to have it here for her when they were still at the resort.

Two steps took her to the sofa. She picked up the parcel and was about to drop it into the trash, but hesitated. Her fingers rasped over the pretty bow, and even though it might not be in her best interest, she gave a little tug. The silk fell away and she lifted the top of the pretty box to find a sexy red bra and panties. She removed them from the white tissue paper and smoothed her fingers over the material. Her glance moved to the slip of white paper and the instructions to wear them to work Monday morning.

Had Quinn intended to show up, to remove them from her body? She touched the warm, buttery leather on her sofa. It was just last week he'd taken her right here. Put her over his knee and disciplined her. A cry lodged in her throat, half of her wanting to be with him again while the other half wanted to run farther away. The constant tug of war on her emotions and her senses was turning her into a mad woman.

She threw the lingerie back into the box and struggled with the lid, slapping the corners with her palm to force it back in place. Giving up on it, she turned to her window, bracing shaking hands on the sill as she struggled to find some semblance of balance. Horns blared on the street below as heavy rain clouds darkened the sky and blackened the pavement—a fitting match for her somber mood.

There was, however, a part of her that was grateful her friends were all free tonight. She'd called them first thing Saturday night after Quinn had dropped her off at her condo. They were anxious to hear the details of her weekend, but the instant they caught the tremor in her voice they knew something had gone terribly wrong. They'd wanted to check in on her, but she just needed time to herself, and instead of explaining it three times over, she convinced them to meet tonight after work. The less she rehashed the events of the night and the way the situation had dredged up memories best left buried, the better.

Giving her head a hard shake to clear it, she pushed away from the window and grabbed her purse from her desk drawer. She slung it over her shoulder and snatched her umbrella from the rack near her door. She turned her lights off, left her office and hurried down the hall to the waiting elevator. A few seconds later, it deposited her on the main floor, and Tim, the building's main security guard, gave her a worried look as she signed out for the night.

"How are you this evening?" he asked. His tone held concern. This wasn't idle chit-chat.

A wave of embarrassment moved through her and her cheeks warmed as she lowered her eyes and scribbled her name on the pad. God, did everyone who played at the resort know what had happened to her? Whatever happened to the rule "what happens at Freedom stays at Freedom"?

She mumbled that she was fine and darted outside. A flick of the switch on her umbrella opened it and she slipped into the stream of people rushing along the sidewalk. Zigzagging through the crowded streets, she hurried to Onyx, her favorite Manhattan cocktail bar. The heavy front door opened just as she reached for it, and she came face to face with fellow lawyer Rick Douglas, a guy she'd dated in the past.

"Rebecca," he said, his smile so bright, his teeth so straight, she couldn't help but think he'd paid for some dentist's summer home. "Where have you been? I haven't seen you around lately."

"Didn't know you were looking." She closed her umbrella and ducked under the overhead awning with him.

He laughed, and his gaze fell from her face, the look in his eyes almost lecherous. "You know, I always loved that smart mouth of yours."

"Oh yeah?" She held back a smart-assed reply. She knew what it really was about her mouth that he loved. Too bad he never reciprocated such favors in the bedroom. Between the sheets it had always been about his needs.

Blue eyes that any other girl would get lost in narrowed in on hers. "Yeah, so where have you been?"

"Busy working," she explained, not about to tell him anything.

His smile widened. "Beautiful and driven. You'll be partner before you know it." He looked over her shoulder. "You alone?"

With the tip of her umbrella, she pointed to the lounge area. "Meeting my friends."

He stepped closer, crowding her. "Then maybe we can meet up for a drink later. I've missed you." He gestured to a restaurant across the street. "I'm meeting a client in a few, but we should be wrapping up around eight."

Her first reaction was to say no. Been there done that. If she wanted an empty experience that let her know something was missing from her life, she'd use her vibrator. But with Quinn out of the picture and the BDSM lifestyle behind her, if she ever wanted to feel a warm body next to her again she'd soon have to settle for someone like Rick, and a sex life that was less than orgasmic.

But as she visualized herself between the sheets with him, her blood turned cold—her body's way of saying it wanted Quinn, and Quinn only. She shivered, crossed her hands over her chest and hugged herself. For some reason Rick took that as an invitation to touch her. He pulled her into his arms and ran his hands up and down her back to create warmth with friction. Too bad all he succeeded in doing was cementing her belief that climbing between the sheets with him would leave her with nothing but a dull, needy ache in the pit of her stomach.

She shook her head, once again wishing she'd never met Quinn, never felt his touch or known the pleasures of submission. She breathed deep and let it out slowly. Honest to God, the man had ruined her for every other.

"Thanks," she said. "But I can't. I'm seeing someone."

Rick's eyes narrowed and he angled his head, those ocean-blue eyes of his moving over her face.

"Oh, I didn't realize." He rolled one shoulder, like he was brushing it off because he didn't believe her. "Well, if things change between now and eight, you know where to find me."

He pulled the door open for her and she slipped inside. She exhaled slowly, fixed her damp hair, then made her way to her friends. From the empty drink glasses in front of the trio, it was clear they'd been there a while.

She dropped into her chair beside Sophie, and three sets of eyes stared at her with unease.

Rebecca couldn't help but laugh, her mood lightening slightly. Either that, or she'd crossed the line from mad to crazy. Quinn was right. She really did have great friends. As ribbons of tension left her body, those three pairs of eyes narrowed in on her.

She held her hands up. "I'm fine."

Directly across from her, Lilliana reached out and grabbed her hand. "Who are you trying to convince of that? Us or you?"

"Quinn better not have hurt you," Sophie said.

Rebecca turned to look at her friend and had never seen such worry in her eyes. If looks could kill and Quinn was anywhere in the vicinity, he would have been dead by now.

She exhaled slowly. "He didn't, but Felix did."

"Felix?" Melanie asked, pushing a cocktail Rebecca's way. "Who's Felix?"

She took a much-needed drink, leaned forward in her chair and told the entire story.

"Oh, my God," Sophie said, putting her hand on Rebecca's back and giving it a rub. "Thank God Quinn got there in time before he…before you were…well, you know."

Eyes still wide with worry, Melanie gestured to the bartender for another round, and Rebecca tagged on, "After that, I came home, and now I'm putting that whole world behind me."

"Wait, when you say whole world, do you mean Quinn too?" Melanie asked.

Rebecca fished the olive from her drink and plopped it into her mouth. "Yes. I mean Quinn too."

"Becs," Melanie began. "I've never seen you so happy before, and the chemistry between you two was off the charts."

"You need more than chemistry to make a relationship work," she said matter-of-factly.

"So you're saying you want a relationship with him then?" Lilliana asked.

"Yes," she answered without thinking, but as soon as that word left her mouth, her head jerked back with startled surprise. "Wait, no." A beat passed and then, "I don't know."

Was it possible that she wanted a real relationship with Quinn? Hadn't she learned to keep a measure of distance because no one ever stayed? That when someone was done with her they tossed her out like she was yesterday's garbage?

"It doesn't matter," she added. "He told me there was no middle ground with him. I want him to be happy, and I can't give him what he wants." She pushed her hair from her face and looked at Melanie. "Enough about me, what have you three been up to?"

Melanie smiled. "Sophie just made partner."

"What!" Rebecca squealed. She turned to Sophie. "Oh my God. Congratulations." She pulled her friend in for a hug. "Here I was monopolizing the conversation when you had something very important to share."

"You weren't monopolizing, and what you had to say was just as important, if not more so." Rebecca's heart squeezed, and she touched her friend's hand. Sophie smiled in return and added, "The firm booked Onyx for a private gathering Friday night. I hope you'll come."

"I wouldn't miss it for the world," Rebecca assured her.

"Don't forget your plus one."

"Plus one?"

"You get to bring a date."

Rebecca shook her head. "I'm coming alone."

"Have you heard from him?" Lilliana asked, turning the conversation back to Rebecca.

"He texts me every day to make sure I'm okay, but he hasn't been by to see me, if that's what you mean."

"Maybe he's giving you space," Melanie suggested.

"Maybe." She straightened in her chair and reached for her drink. "Or maybe we're just finished and he's only checking on me because he's worried I'll sue him after what happened. I mean, our firm did sue him last year and we won."

Clearly not buying that, Sophie leaned toward her and placed her hand over Rebecca's. "I have a question."

"What?" Rebecca turned to her friend. She took in the seriousness on her friend's face and braced herself. Sophie was about to challenge her.

"BDSM is about trust, right?"

"How do you know that?" Melanie asked, her brow wagging. Mel winked at Rebecca and Rebecca forced a smile. Each friend was dealing with this situation differently. While Sophie went the stern route, Melanie chose the playful. She loved her for that, but wasn't in a laughing mood.

"I did a bit of research," Sophie explained. As her friends continued to stare at her she took a sip of her drink and said, "What? I was curious."

Rebecca eyed her friend. "What are you getting at?"

"Did you ever stop to think that maybe Quinn feels guilty?"

"Guilty?"

Sophie took a sip of her martini. "I only met him briefly, but he strikes me as the kind of guy who'd hold himself responsible for this."

Rebecca recalled the rage in his eyes, and how he'd left Felix for dead. "Maybe, but it wasn't his fault."

"If you don't hold him personally responsible, then why can't you continue to have a relationship with him?"

"Because I'm done dabbling in that lifestyle." Everyone at the table went silent, waiting for her to continue. "Look, it's like this, a leopard can't change its spots. Quinn is who he is and I would never ask him to change for me. I want him to be happy and he won't be able to find that happiness with me."

"You're right," Melanie said. "A leopard can't change its spots." She paused, jabbed her finger in the air toward Rebecca and added, "What you fail to see in that old adage is that it applies to you too."

Rebecca eyed her over the rim of her martini glass. "What do you mean?"

"He introduced you to a world you liked, right?" Melanie said.

"Yeah, but—"

Melanie cut her off. "Do you think you can just go back to vanilla sex after that? You were so completely and utterly bored with the men in your life, Becs. Quinn changed that for you."

She set her glass down. "I can't." The olives collided, splashing gin over the side. She grabbed a napkin and wiped her stemware before adding, "I can't go back to that. Felix put a blindfold on me, Melanie. That was a hard limit for me."

Lilliana squeezed her hand. "I'm sorry, honey. I really am. But it was Felix who did that, not Quinn."

Rebecca blew out a breath. "I know but…" She knew her friends were trying to help, but what they failed to understand was the significance of the blindfold, or how her foster mother used the dark, rat-infested basement to punish an innocent child. If she stepped back into that lifestyle something horrible could happen again.

Her stomach knotted as she thought about the woman who claimed to be taking care of her because she cared about her well-being. What Dorothy Kean really cared about was the money she received in return for providing a roof over Rebecca's head. The second Rebecca turned eighteen and Dorothy could no longer collect government funds, she'd tossed her out the door.

Rebecca was glad to go. She'd never had any intention of staying in the abusive household once she was of legal age anyway. From that day forward she'd worked two jobs, sometimes three, to put herself through college. She'd met these three wonderful women she called her closest friends when she went to work at the firm a few years ago, and had never once revealed her abusive past. They had no idea how hard it was for her to be blindfolded, how the darkness had suffocated her, choked her until she couldn't breathe.

Her hand went to her chest, and she could feel the room closing in on her as her heart pounded against her ribcage. She took another drink to wash away the anxiety rising in her throat.

"I think you should give him another chance," Sophie said quietly.

"The only way I could do that is if he left that lifestyle behind, and like I already said, I would never ask that because I care about his happiness."

Just then, her cell phone pinged. She swiped her thumb over the screen and her pulse leapt when she read the message.

"Is it Quinn?" Sophie asked.

She nodded. "Yeah."

"What does he want?"

"To see me."

"Don't you think you should at least talk to him, see what he wants?" Melanie asked. "Maybe he's ready to give it all up for you."

"I told you, I'd never want him to do that…"

Melanie looked past her shoulder, and when her eyes went big, Rebecca's words fell off. She didn't need to turn around to know Quinn was standing there. She could feel him long before she could see him. A beat passed, then she pushed from the table. The scraping sound her chair made as she turned broke the sudden, uneasy silence of her friends, and when she twisted and caught the uncertainly in the eyes of the masterful Dom, the world around her went a little fuzzy around the edges.

"Quinn," she managed to get out past the lump in her throat. Her glance left his face to take in his rumpled shirt and the wrinkles in his pants. How long had he been sleeping in them? She took in the deep lines around his eyes, the scruff on his chin. Her heart squeezed with the need to go to him and make it better. But she rooted herself, forcing herself not to smooth the worry from his brow, kiss away the grim line of dejection on his mouth. Reaching out to him meant going back to his lifestyle, and that was out of the question. "You shouldn't be here."

"Rebecca," he whispered, his voice cracked and raspy, like he'd just swallowed a handful of nails. "This is exactly where I should be."

"Quinn, no…"

The tender way he looked at her dissolved her words. He dropped to his knees beside her, and she took in the tension in his body as he cupped her face. His fingers tightened with care. "I need you to come with me. We need to talk."

Three

Quinn took Rebecca's hand in his, ignoring the buzzing phone in his pocket. His brother had been calling for days, but Quinn was in no shape to talk to him. The only one he wanted to speak with was Rebecca. He was desperate to make things right between them.

He turned to her friends. "You ladies don't mind if I steal Rebecca away for a few minutes, do you?"

"No," they all said in unison. He nodded, feeling a degree of relief. At least her friends weren't trying to convince her to stay away from him. Although, after what she'd been through at the resort, he wouldn't blame them if they were.

Rebecca opened her mouth to speak, but he put his finger to her lips. "I'm sorry, Rebecca. I'm so goddamn sorry. You have to believe me."

She shifted in her chair. "Quinn…" Her voice sounded different, defeated.

Refusing to let her push him from her life without at least hearing him out, he rushed out with, "I take all the blame, and if you'll give me a chance I'll make this right between us. No matter what it takes, I'll make it right."

Her face softened. "It's not your fault, Quinn. Felix tricked me into going to the castle. Neither of us could have known what he had planned."

The world crushed in on him, his thoughts reeling from the emotional whiplash he'd been suffering since finding her blindfolded and tied to that fucking cross. He brought her hand to his mouth and just held it there as he worked to pull himself together. He squeezed slightly, and said, "It *is* my fault. I'm a man of my word and I asked for your trust. I promised I'd respect it. You gave it to me freely, and I let you down." He breathed deep, his nostrils flaring as he pulled in the warm, sweet scent of her skin. "I let both of us down."

Her friends pushed away from the table. "We'll leave you two alone," Sophie said.

Rebecca held her hand up to stop them and Quinn's heart sank. She was a strong-willed woman—it was one of the things he loved about her—but she needed to hear him out. She'd come to mean so much to him and if she pushed him out of her life now, Quinn had no idea what he'd do.

"You three stay. We'll go."

Overwhelmed with relief, his knees gave a little as he stood and pulled her up with him. "My driver's waiting. We can go anywhere you want. Anywhere you feel safe."

She nodded and when they turned to go, she banged into some guy looking at her in a lewd way that fired Quinn's blood.

"Rebecca," the guy said, putting his hand on her shoulder. "I finished my meeting early and thought I'd come see if you changed your mind."

Quinn put his arm around her waist and pulled her to him to lay claim. The guy's hand fell from her shoulder and his eyes narrowed.

"Rick," she said, "This is Quinn. Quinn, this is Rick. He's my…an old friend."

A half smirk lingered on Rick's face. "An old friend?"

When she didn't respond, he stuck his hand out and met Quinn's glance. "Are you an old friend too?" he asked.

"No," was all Quinn said as he gave the man's hand a hard shake.

"So I guess you really are seeing someone," Rick said. "My loss."

Quinn pulled her closer, ready to piss a circle around Rebecca if Rick didn't back the fuck off.

Rick smiled at Rebecca, like Quinn was of no importance, and touched a loose tendril of her hair when he said, "I guess I'll see you here Friday night then."

Quinn's jaw seesawed from side to side, ready to tell Rick to stop fucking touching her, but the last thing Rebecca needed was more violence, or for him to make a scene.

Rebecca frowned and went quiet for a moment. A second later, she glanced back up at Rick, her eyes wide like a light bulb had gone off. "Right, Sophie's party."

Struggling to keep his anger in check as the asshole blatantly made a play for Rebecca in front of him, Quinn sucked in a quick breath to keep his shit together. He looked Rebecca over and read her body language: lashes blinking rapidly, weight shifting from one foot to the other, body far too tense. As unease poured off her in waves, his protective instincts kicked in. He put his hand on the small of her back to remove her from the situation. Whether she wanted to be with him or not, it wasn't going to stop him from taking care of her.

"Ready?" he asked. She nodded and grabbed her purse and umbrella. Quinn maneuvered them around Rick and made their way to the front door. Once outside he called for his car and stood under the awning with her as the rain pounded the pavement.

She didn't have to answer, and he wasn't going to push, but he couldn't help but ask, "Who's Rick and what's going on Friday night?"

"He's a friend, and Friday night is a celebration. Sophie made partner."

"Good for her. Why does Rick make you uncomfortable?"

Her lips thinned and she folded her arms across her chest. "You didn't have to go all alpha on him."

Did she have no idea how protective he was of her or the measures he'd take to ensure her safety? "You think that was going alpha?"

"Yes."

Quinn put his hands on her shoulders and looked deep into her eyes. Behind the blue he saw that wall again. One she'd put up for protection and he couldn't get past.

"Let me just say this. If he ever touches you again, you'll really see me go alpha."

"Actually, I already have," she said so quietly he had to strain to hear her.

Her body visually shivered as she looked away. "Look at me," he said. She instantly obliged, the sweet submissive in her responding to his command. He cupped her face. "I'm sorry. I promised you I'd always see to your safety, and I failed." He looked back into the lounge, watching Rick from afar. "I won't fail again."

"Quinn…"

His car pulled up to the curb and he stepped to the sidewalk to open the door. She hesitated for a moment and rain poured down his face as he waited. "All I want to do is talk. Any time you say you want to leave, my driver will take you home. I promise you that."

She nodded and he let loose a breath of relief as she slid in. His phone buzzed again as he slipped in next to her. He ignored it and asked, "Where to?"

"My place."

She gave the driver the address, then sank back next to him. Quinn took her hand and shifted to face her. The unsure look in her eyes gave him pause. If he wanted her to trust him, he'd have to change tactics.

"How about we start again."

"Quinn, I'm not interested in playing in that lifestyle again," she said quickly, a slight quiver to her voice.

"I know," he said in a bid to relax her. "I'm not asking you to. What I'm asking is for you to be my friend."

Her head came back with a start. "Friend? After what we've done, you think we can just forget it all and be friends?"

"Sure."

"You mean friends with benefits, right?"

"Of course I want sex, Rebecca, but I want to give you space, start fresh. I want everything that happens to be your choice, your call. I want you, and will do whatever it takes to have you, but every choice has to be yours, every single move is based on your terms this time."

She went quiet for a long time, and then said, "My terms mean doing things the way I normally would. Like hanging out, going to the movies, eating dinner. And when it comes to sex…well, I guess that would mean vanilla, no dungeon."

No BDSM. He got it. "I can do all that."

She shook her head. "But I'd never ask you to change. I'd never want you to. You deserve to have the things you want."

"You're not asking, I'm offering. It's what I want."

She turned and stared out the window. He watched her, letting her digest what he was asking. It'd kill him to be around her without dominating her, but he'd have to find a way. She needed that from him. If giving up the lifestyle was what it took to gain her trust and show her how much he cared about her and her needs, then he'd damn well do it.

"So can we start again?" he pushed. "Friends. Your terms."

Her eyes met his, and she smiled as she pulled her hand from his to place it on her lap. "Friends don't hold hands in the backseat of a car," she said.

He exhaled slowly. "So that's a yes?"

"Yes, we can be friends. If that's what you want."

He touched her chin and drew it back to him. "I told you I'd always be honest, so the truth is, what I want is to tie you up and possess you, physically and mentally, but I can't…*won't*…put you through that."

Her body shook. She might be walking away from the lifestyle, but it didn't mean she was no longer a sub. He'd awakened that part of her and now it existed whether she wanted it to or not.

"Okay," she said quietly.

"So…" he began. "What do you want to do tonight?"

"Before we do anything, I think you should answer your phone. It's been ringing all night."

"Right." Quinn fished his phone from his pocket. He slid his finger across the screen and his brother's number popped up. "Hey, Josh, what's up?"

"That's what I was going to ask you. I haven't heard from you in days. Neither have Dean and Gabe."

"Been busy." It was a half-truth. He'd been agonizing over Rebecca for days and had ignored their calls on purpose. He loved his brothers more than life, but damned if they knew how to mind their own business. They'd be in New York in a flash if they thought Quinn was in any kind of trouble. Then again, he'd be on the next plane to

L.A. if the situation was reversed and his calls were going unanswered.

His brother went quiet for a moment, and Quinn cringed. Jesus, he wished his twin couldn't read him so well. "Doing what?" Josh asked.

"None of your business, little brother." Okay, so Quinn might have been born only one minute before Josh, but he never let his twin forget it.

"I know when something is wrong, bro."

"Have you come off your meds again?"

Rebecca chuckled, and Quinn grinned at her.

"Fuck off," Josh said, the worry in his voice lightening as he laughed. "I was just about to jump on the next plane and check on you."

"While I would like to see you, nothing is wrong and you don't have to check on me." Wanting to turn the focus off him, he asked, "How's Mom?"

They talked for a few more minutes, and when the car pulled up to the curb in front of Rebecca's place, she opened her door.

"Listen, bro, I have to go. Tell the guys I'm fine. Talk to you soon." He powered his phone down, slid from the car and met Rebecca on the sidewalk. He put his arm around her back and she eyed him.

"What?" he asked. "Friends do that."

She rolled her eyes and fished her key ring from her purse. "So that was your younger brother."

"Yeah. Josh."

"He was worried about you." She went quiet for a moment, thoughtful, then added, "He sounds nice."

"He's not nice. He's a pain in my ass."

She laughed softly and he followed her into her condo. He looked around when she flipped her lights on.

"Nice place," he said.

"It's home." She led him to the living room and he gave the room a once over.

He took in the artwork on her walls and admired the paintings. "You have great taste." As he appreciated her belongings, he looked for something more personal. Family was important to the Montgomerys and his mother made sure Quinn had memorabilia when he'd moved to the East Coast. He sat on the sofa. "No brothers and sisters?"

"Not that I know of. Like I said, I never knew my mother."

"What happened to her?"

"I have no idea." She pointed toward the hall and he could tell she was trying to redirect the conversation. "I'm going to get changed. Why don't you find us a movie to watch?"

Right. A movie. That was what she'd normally do.

"Okay." He grabbed the remote and pressed the power button. He listened to her heels on the wood floors as she disappeared down the hall. He flicked through the channels, fighting an internal battle to go to her. He'd promised her friendship, to let her call the shots, but it warred with the need that sang in his veins.

He dropped the remote, and under the guise of finding the bathroom, he walked down the hall. Rustling sounds of her removing her clothes came from her bedroom, and he kept his distance, his body on fire as he visualized her naked on her knees before him. Shit. He clenched his teeth and cursed under his breath, determined to keep that side of himself in check.

He raked a shaky hand through his hair, and just as he was about to do a one-eighty and make his way back to the sofa, she came from her room and crashed into him.

"Oh," she said, surprise in her eyes.

He wrapped his arm around her waist and splayed his hands over the T-shirt and pajama pants she'd changed into as he tugged her up against him. "Sorry."

"What…what were you doing?" Her body pressed against his and the heat they generated was enough to light an entire New York block.

"Looking for the bathroom."

She looked over his shoulder. "You passed it."

"I know."

He dipped his head, his lips so close to hers he could taste her sweet breath. His heart pounded with the urge to take her. One kiss. One quick little kiss was all he needed to get him through the night. He was sure of it. He dipped his head, unable to help himself.

"Quinn…" she said breathlessly as his lips hovered over hers. "What are you doing?"

Her words snapped some sense back in to him. He stepped back before he ruined what he was trying to do. *Get it together, Montgomery. She's calling the shots.*

"Fuck. I'm sorry. I just…"

Desire reflected in her eyes and he knew she wanted this every bit as much as he did. But he'd promised to back off, and he intended to keep his words. If she wanted sex, she'd have to initiate it.

She shook her head and stepped back. "You can't do this, Quinn. You can't do vanilla. And you shouldn't have to try."

Worry ripped through him. He couldn't lose her again. He reached for her elbow to bring her back. "Yes, I can. I want to."

She pulled farther away from him and lowered her head. "You're a good man, and you deserve someone who can give you what you really want."

Quinn stepped closer to her, put his fingers under her chin and lifted until her eyes met his. "Rebecca, what I really want is you and I can do this. I'll never ask for anything you can't give."

Four

Even though every alarm bell was ringing, warning her to walk away from this—from Quinn—her brain was no longer calling the shots. Her body ached for him, craved him in a way she couldn't quite put into words.

She looked into his eyes and the heat she met there fired the needy spot between her legs. *I'll never ask for anything you can't give.* Was it possible that he could check the Dom at the door and engage in vanilla sex with her?

But wasn't it the Dom in him that attracted her in the first place?

Regardless, that was a path she wouldn't—couldn't—walk again. No way could she engage in activities that unearthed her dark past.

"I want…" She stopped speaking. If she started this, it would be on her. He'd asked for friendship to start, and what she did next would determine the amount of intimacy involved in the early stages of said friendship. But she'd missed him too much and was too fired up to think past tonight. Maybe she wouldn't. Maybe she'd just concentrate on how much she needed to feel him inside her right now.

His nostrils flared. "Tell me what you want, Rebecca."

"What if I said I wanted friends *with* benefits to start?"

"Then that's what I'll give you."

He cupped her elbow and drew her close, until her body was pressed against his. Sexual tension flared between them as his touch went right through her.

"You once said there was no middle of the road."

"That was before."

"Is changing even possible?" she asked, wondering if *she* could go back to vanilla after experiencing his brand of lovemaking. "Is it possible for us to do vanilla in the bedroom after what we've been through?"

"Let's find out."

His mouth came down over hers again, and his tongue slipped inside. He kissed her long and deep, then picked her up and carried her to her room. He placed her on the edge of the bed and her T-shirt rode up a tiny bit to expose her flat stomach.

His eyes darkened when his gaze dropped and she sensed he was fighting an internal battle. He briefly closed his eyes and pinched the bridge of his nose.

"Quinn." God, could they really do this?

He opened his eyes and reached for the buttons on his shirt. "Yeah," he said, his voice so deep it sent quivers through her. Her train of thought derailed when he removed his shirt to expose his muscular body. Her mouth watered and her hands itched to touch him. She sat still, taking in all his beautiful nakedness as he kicked off his shoes and ripped open his pants. He pulled them off, along with his boxers, and kicked them away.

His cock sprang to life, and she reached out and closed her fingers around it. He groaned and all she could think about was dropping to her knees. Instead, she focused on the texture and hard length of him, and when he stepped closer, she wrapped her lips around his cock, drawing it deep into her mouth.

His hands gripped her hair and he tugged. Her head jerked back and her breath caught. Was he crossing into Dom territory? As if catching himself, a groan sounded in his throat and he let go of her hair to slide his fingers around the back of her head. He held her and followed the motion as she drew him in and out, licking her tongue over the crown with each passing.

Pre-come pooled on his crown and she moaned with pleasure as she lapped it. Quinn made a noise that sounded like he was in complete agony, then pulled his cock from her mouth. He dropped to his knees in front of her and his glance met hers. The intensity in his gaze sucked the oxygen from her lungs. She swallowed—hard—as he gripped the band of her pajama bottoms and pulled them off. Her T-shirt and bra came next, and he tossed them on to the top of the pile, leaving her only in her panties. He gripped her inner thighs, his fingers biting into her skin hard enough to leave bruises as he widened them. Was this his way of marking her, claiming her without the ties that bind? His breath whispered over her thighs, then he pressed his nose against her skin and breathed her in.

He gave her an easy shove and she fell backward onto the mattress. Warm fingers slid along her thighs until they reached her panties. He toyed with them for a moment, rubbing the material between his thumb and index finger. He opened his mouth, then closed it again. Was he contemplating a reprimand for having them on? Much to her dismay, a thrill moved through her. He slowly slid the slip of material down her legs and removed them. His jaw clenched, and while he was exercising extreme restraint, there was a part of her that wanted him to lose it, to take control, be the man he really was.

His head dipped. She bit her lip at that first sweet touch of his tongue. He stroked from bottom to top, circling her clit until she was nearly delirious with want.

She gripped the sheets beneath her and held on as he took possession of her sex. That's when she realized she was lying perfectly still, the way her Dom had always instructed.

That thought flew from her mind when he inserted a finger. His warm breath whispered over her wet sex with a growl of approval. With his finger still inside her, he slid over her body. His mouth found hers and his kiss was full of passion when their lips collided. His cock pressed against the side of her stomach as he pulled his hand from between her legs to capture hers wrists. He shoved her arms above her head, holding them in one hand as he repositioned himself until his cock teased her opening. His other hand pushed into the bed beside her head, and the next thing she knew he was thrusting inside her.

She moved with him, her pelvis banging against his, and as they came together her heart swelled. She'd missed this. Missed him.

His mouth came down hard and she tugged until she freed one hand, needing to touch him. Thick muscles jumped beneath her roaming hand and he cursed under his breath. She sucked in air, loving how he reacted to her touch. But as much as she wanted him in her bed, she didn't want to hold him back from what he really needed. His hand slipped between their bodies and her thoughts fragmented as he applied pressure to her clit.

She closed her eyes, reveling in the sensations. He brought her higher and higher, until an orgasm was only a breath away. A cry lodged in her throat.

"That's it, kitten. Come for me."

The second she heard her pet name roll off his tongue, she gave herself over to her orgasm. Her muscles spasmed, clenched around his thickness, the tension in her body easing.

"So good," she murmured, squeezing tighter.

Quinn positioned both hands beside her head, holding them there as he drove so fast and deep she feared the bed was going to break. He pounded harder than ever before, the way he was taking her far more intense than anything she'd ever felt. His eyes searched hers, and she wiggled one hand free to put her palm on his cheeks. His gaze bore into hers and when she saw the want…need…the responsibly he was shouldering, the pain he was carrying, her heart squeezed.

"Quinn," she murmured. Tears pricked her eyes. She loved him for wanting to be what she needed, but it wasn't fair to him. Why should he be punished for something Felix had done?

He threw his head back and growled as he jettisoned his seed high inside her. He collapsed on top of her, perspiration sealing them as one. His heart pounded against her chest as they both struggled to breathe. He buried his face in her neck and she held him to her, running her fingers though his damp hair.

"Hey," he said. He lifted his head, his eyes meeting hers. He frowned and looked her over. "Something on your mind?"

She swallowed against the tightness in her throat. "We can't do this."

His brow furrowed. "Rebecca, don't."

She touched his face. "I know you think you can, but it's not who you are, and you shouldn't change for anyone."

"You're not just anyone."

Her heart ached. "Quinn—"

"It's what I want."

She nodded, but unease crept through her. He was trying to be something he wasn't. Sooner or later he'd see that, and then they'd have no choice but to go their separate ways. Her whole life people had left her. She cared about this man, and each minute with him, she was falling more and more in love. How would she ever handle him walking out of her life?

He rolled and pulled her onto his chest. She cuddled into him and he drew up the blankets. He adjusted his pillow and sank farther into it.

"Damn," he murmured and started to get up.

"Where are you going?" she asked.

"To get the bathroom light."

"Leave it on."

"You sleep with the light on?"

"I don't really like the dark," she explained.

He shifted until he faced her and tucked her hair behind her ears. "What is it about the dark that frightens you?"

Instead of answering, she said, "We should get some sleep. I have a busy day tomorrow." She rolled onto her back and fixed the blankets around her.

He went up on one elbow. "Rebecca?"

"Yeah," she said quietly.

"If you didn't know your mom, who raised you?"

"I was in foster care," she said quietly. "I was tossed around a lot and raised by many different people. It wasn't so bad…until I hit thirteen," she said. A shiver moved through her and she wondered why she was sharing something so personal.

"What happened when you were thirteen?" he asked.

Rebecca stared at the ceiling, her heart pounding wildly. She'd always tried to be so good, hoping one of the *nice* families would keep her, but they never did. "What happened, Rebecca?"

"They stopped moving me. I stayed in the same place until I was eighteen."

He gripped her hips and rolled her toward him, and when she caught the tenderness on his face, her heart missed a beat.

He ran the backs of his fingers over her cheek. "I'm sorry."

"It's okay, it's behind me."

His eyes moved over her face, and she wished he couldn't read her so well.

"That must have been hard. It's not normal for a little girl to grow up without a mom."

A deep sadness entered his eyes, and, wanting to wipe it away, she forced a smile and said, "Nothing about me is normal, Quinn."

He pressed his forehead to hers. In a breathless whisper, he said, "We'll do normal, Rebecca. We'll do normal because that's what you need."

Five

Quinn dropped Rebecca off at work, and, after kissing her for a good twenty minutes, he made his way home. He let himself in and when he heard a familiar voice coming from his den, he walked down the hall to find his baby brother, Josh, with his feet on Quinn's desk, chatting loudly on his cell phone.

Quinn folded his arms and glared at his brother, even though he could never really be mad at him. "Come on in. Make yourself at home."

"Gotta go," Josh said into the phone, then dropped it onto Quinn's desk. A smile spread across his face. He climbed to his feet, arms wide as he crossed the room. "Hey, big bro."

"I told you I was fine," Quinn said, making his voice hard even though he was happy to see his brother. He gave him a hug, holding him a little longer than necessary. It was a twin thing. They were always able to sense when one needed the other, able to give comfort the way no one else could.

Josh eyed him. "You don't look fine."

"Then I guess you must not either, considering we look the same."

"You know what I mean."

Quinn exhaled and crossed the room. He plunked himself down on his leather chair just as Eloise, the head of his staff, came in with a fresh pot of coffee and a plate of muffins.

Josh gave her a smile and she practically fluttered out of the room. "Leave my staff alone," Quinn said. He shook his head at his brother's antics. Jesus, they might be twins, but Josh, a brilliant software analyst out in Silicon Valley, was like a damn magician when it came to the opposite sex. One look from him and women's panties disappeared.

Even his elderly, *married*, caretaker wasn't immune to his brother's charms.

"So I take it you heard?" Quinn asked. It was only a matter of time before the news of what had happened to Rebecca, and Felix's removal from the island, would trickle through the grapevine and reach his brother's club out in California.

"Yeah. Is she okay?"

He scrubbed his chin, in desperate need of a shave. "Not really."

"What are you going to do?"

"I'm going to quit the lifestyle."

Josh planted himself on the edge of Quinn's desk and doctored a coffee. "You're kidding, right?"

"No, I'm not. I'm in love with her, Josh."

Josh gestured toward the velvet box with the diamond collar inside. The piece he'd called a friend to commission when he was at the resort.

"I take it that was for her, then?"

Desperate for caffeine, Quinn took a drink from his cup and set it on a coaster. "*Was*, yes. But not anymore."

"And you think you can just—" Josh paused and snapped his fingers, "—turn off that side of yourself."

"I don't have a choice. Felix scared her, and now she doesn't want any part of the lifestyle. If I want to be with her, it's what I have to do." He recalled the blindfold, and something buzzed in the back of his brain. Jesus, Rebecca had that same distant look on her face, the same lost look in her eyes, when he asked about her upbringing. The two had to go hand-in-hand. He knew she'd told him something very private, something he assumed she'd never shared with many, and while he wanted her to trust him with her secrets, he had no choice but to use the information if he wanted to help her.

Josh peeled the paper off a muffin. "Felix is an asshole."

"I know. I talked to his father, and he was furious. We won't be seeing him around the resort anytime soon."

His brother turned serious. "The lifestyle aside, Quinn. You know our past. You think you can be loyal to one woman?"

Since meeting her, she was all he'd been able to think about. "I'm not my father. I'm my own man, and it's time I realized that. You too."

Josh went quiet, thoughtful, then he grinned. "So, when do I get to meet this girl who's got my brother whipped? Or rather, not whipped."

"Very funny. And for the record, you're the one who likes to get whipped, not me."

"True." He nodded and chewed on his muffin. "So when do I get to meet her?" he asked again.

"This weekend. There's a party for one of her friends who just made partner at the firm."

"Cool. Are you able to take a few days off, spend some time with your favorite bro while I'm in town?"

"There's nothing I'd like better." He booted up his computer and did a search on Rebecca Andrews. "But first I need to do a bit of work."

Josh grabbed his phone. "I have a few calls to make myself, anyway."

His brother sauntered out of the office. Once he was out of earshot, Quinn picked up his phone and called an old friend. It rang twice, then Mike picked up.

"Mike, it's Quinn. How are you?"

"Better than you."

"What makes you say that?" Quinn asked.

"Because you're calling me." He laughed, a big boom of a sound that fit the man's personality. "Who is she, and what do you need to know?"

Quinn grinned. Mike was the best private investigator in the city, and if he couldn't find out about Rebecca's past, no one could. "Rebecca Andrews, and everything you've got on her."

He hung up and made his way to the shower, desperate for a shave and a change of clothes. After cleaning up, he met his brother in the den. His phone pinged as he entered and he grabbed it from his desk. He checked the name and swiped the screen.

"That was fast," he said.

"When you're the best, you're the best," Mike said, laughing. Then his voice dropped, became serious. "I have the information you're looking for."

Quinn grabbed a pen and jotted down an address. He spoke to Mike for a few more minutes, then ended the call and looked at his brother. "Want to go for a drive?"

* * *

With Sophie's party in full swing, Melanie popped an olive into her mouth, her eyes opening wide as she looked past Rebecca's shoulders. "Am I seeing double or is that guy Quinn's twin?"

"Maybe you had one too many of these," Lilliana teased, gesturing to Melanie's empty glass.

Rebecca's body buzzed to life, the way it always did when Quinn was near. She turned in her chair and her mouth dropped when she saw Quinn walking into Onyx with a man who looked just like him.

"He never told me Josh was his twin," she said, smoothing her hand over her skirt.

"Dibs," Melanie yelled over the cacophony of sounds in the lounge, and the girls all laughed.

"Hey, it's Sophie's night," Lilliana said. "She gets to call dibs first." She wagged her eyebrows. "That is, if she wants."

They all looked at Sophie and she grinned. "Oh, she wants."

"Damn," Melanie said, and Lilliana nudged her. "He did say he had three brothers, one for all of us."

Melanie's smile returned. "You're right. He's all yours, Sophie."

As her friends discussed their dating options, Rebecca watched the way Quinn commanded the room, the way all the women responded to him and his brother as they cut through the crowd. The two oozed rugged sex appeal and testosterone as they made their way toward her table. She looked them over and admired their perfectly cut suits that showcased their athletic bodies. Rebecca shifted in her chair and squeezed her legs tighter. Honest to God, ovaries had to be bursting all over the lounge tonight.

She hadn't seen him since he'd slept over at her apartment earlier in the week and knew it was because his brother was in town.

"I thought you weren't going to invite him," Sophie said.

"I didn't." She might not have invited him, but there was a part of her that expected him to show, especially after Rick's parting comment about seeing her Friday night. Rebecca toyed with the top button on her blouse and remembered what she was wearing under her skirt, or rather what she wasn't wearing. Even though Quinn had insisted they do things the vanilla way, she cared about him and wanted to do something just for him.

Quinn's eyes met hers, and the smile fell from his face. Her heart skipped. Why the hell was he so tense? As anger poured off him in waves and undulated toward her, a hand landed on her shoulder and she turned to see Rick standing over her.

"How about a dance?" he asked, looking at her in that familiar, wolfish way that made her feel cold inside.

"I…I…" As Quinn closed the distance, she couldn't seem to keep her thoughts focused. The things that man could do to her without even trying was downright ridiculous.

"She's with me," Quinn said, his jaw seesawing as he glared at Rick.

Rick shrugged. "Hey, it's just a dance."

Quinn's glance dropped to Rebecca's shoulder. His nostrils flared and in a voice that belied the tension in his body, he said calmly, "Take your hand off her."

In a show of allegiance, his brother stepped up beside him. "Everything okay?"

Rick hesitated for a moment, laser eyes going back and forth between the two brothers, then removed his hand. Smart move.

"I need a drink," he said, and disappeared into the crowd.

Rebecca opened her mouth and closed it again, and Quinn's face softened the way it always did when he turned to her.

"Quinn," she began, not knowing whether to thank him or punch him.

He put his mouth close to her ear. "I don't like the way he looks at you."

"You can't go around scaring people off. It's not...*normal*."

"I'm sorry. I just...it's in my nature to protect you, Rebecca. I'm afraid that's not something I can change."

"It's not something you should change," she said softly.

That brought a smile to his face. He looked at her friends, his gaze stopping on Sophie. "I hear congratulations are in order."

Sophie smiled. "Thanks."

"And I see you brought her a gift," Melanie piped in, much to Rebecca's mortification. Rebecca glared at her, but the comment didn't seem to bother either Montgomery brother.

Without missing a beat, Quinn said, "This is Josh. My little brother."

"Little?" Melanie questioned. She blatantly looked him over, her gaze lingering a little too far south.

Rebecca was just about to kick her under the table when Josh laughed.

"Don't worry. Not in the ways that count," Josh teased, his smile so devilish and charming, if her friends had tails they'd all be wagging.

"Aren't you twins?" Lilliana asked.

"Yeah, Quinn was born one minute before me, and thinks he wears the Montgomery crown because of it."

Quinn laughed and turned his attention to Rebecca. He reached for her hand. "Dance with me." She stood and without wasting a second, Melanie waved her hand toward Rebecca's now-empty chair.

"Have a seat, little brother," she said.

"You okay, bro?" Quinn asked.

Josh sat down and gestured for the bartender. "I think I'm in pretty good hands."

Quinn turned to Rebecca. "They're going to eat him alive, aren't they?"

"Like sharks. But something tells me your brother can handle himself."

Quinn laughed and led Rebecca to the small dance floor. He pulled her into his arms and she melted against him. She'd missed him so much this week. Missed his touches, his kisses, the way he made her feel like the most important woman in the world.

"Still friends?" he asked.

"After that stunt with Rick, I'm not so sure you should get any benefits."

"I don't like him."

She crinkled her nose. "Truthfully, neither do I. He's always groping."

"Stay with me tonight," he said, catching her off guard.

"What?" she asked.

"Friends sleep over."

Her body warmed. "What about your brother?"

Quinn angled his head and looked at Josh. "He's a big boy."

"So I heard."

"But remember, I'm bigger."

Unable to help herself, she laughed out loud. She put her hand over her mouth when she the attention she was drawing.

He pulled her hand away and, in a commanding move, held them behind her back. "Don't. I love your laugh."

He pulled her in tighter, and she enjoyed the feel of his hard body against hers. When the song ended they made their way back to the table and spent the remainder of the night chatting as members of the law firm came up to congratulate Sophie. She saw Quinn check his watch, then caught Sophie's eye. She wanted to be alone with Quinn, but didn't want to leave her friend's party.

As if sensing her dilemma, Sophie came to her rescue. "Thanks for coming. It was good to see you both tonight. Let's catch up over lunch next week." Rebecca gave her friend a smile full of thanks.

Quinn stood and put his hand on his brother's shoulder. "You coming?"

"Eventually." He picked up his full bottle of beer.

"I'll see you later then."

Quinn guided Rebecca out the door, and after they climbed into the backseat of his car, Quinn instructed the driver to take them to his place.

A few minutes later she was walking the long hallway of Quinn's home, but the second she entered his bedroom, she noticed the scarves on his nightstand—ones he'd given her as a gift then used to tie her up with. Her body quivered, but Quinn must have mistaken it for unease.

He hurried across the room, gathered them both into his hands and placed them back in the box—a box that reminded her of the red silk panties and bra he'd sent to her office.

"You forgot to take them home with you," he said.

She nodded, her glance going to the bedposts in remembrance. Quinn stepped up to her, brushed his thumb over her mouth and whispered, "Normal," before he pressed his lips to hers.

Six

The sweet taste of her mouth was almost more than he could take. He fought the overwhelming urge to dominate her, to see her on her knees, to feel the sweet victory of her submission. But the only way he'd want her bowing before him was if she had willingly fallen to her knees. Since he couldn't—wouldn't—go there with her, he sucked in a quick breath to fuel his brain and keep himself on track. He'd insisted on doing things the way she normally would and he damn well intended to stick to that plan. Even if it killed him.

She slid her hands around him and kissed him back, the soft noises in her throat driving him mad. His hands left her face and traveled down her arms, and while he wanted to pin them behind her back he resisted the urge and shifted his focus.

"You're overdressed," he murmured, reaching for the small buttons on her blouse.

"You are too." She pushed at the lapels on his suit jacket, forcing it from his shoulders, and he growled as her fingers raced over him.

It had been all he could do to keep his distance this week, to give her the space she needed, but now, well, now that he had her all to himself, he couldn't wait another second to have her naked on his bed.

He popped the buttons on her blouse and peeled it open. When he saw her in black lace, lust rocketed through him. While he loved her in black, he was dying to see her in the red lace he'd sent to her office last week. With a quick flick, he unhooked her bra, and she let loose a little breathy whisper as he bared her breasts.

He ran his thumb over her nipples, making them harder. They formed tight peaks, and he dipped his head to draw one into his mouth. He licked and sucked, but as need consumed him, he teetered on the edge of sanity. He bit down with force, unable to help himself.

She gasped and it snapped some sense back into him. He eased off, brushing his tongue over her hard nubs to soften the sting. His gaze darted to hers, and he saw the ecstasy flittering across her face. Jesus. Her head fell forward, her hair spilling over her bare shoulders. Christ, seeing her like that, seeing the need on her face brought the Dom back to the surface, demanding that he tie her to the bedposts and take her hard.

He dipped a hand under her skirt and caressed her inner thighs. She widened her legs for him and his hand traveled higher, to stroke her hot core. The second he reached the juncture between her legs, air left his lungs in a whoosh and the room nearly closed in on him.

"Jesus, Rebecca," he bit out. His hand stilled near her pussy, the tension in him escalating as she came to him the way he loved. "You're not wearing panties."

"Is that a problem?" she asked. She blinked up at him, the innocent sensuality in her eyes contradicting her actions. Deep down she wanted him to take charge, whether she wanted to admit it or not.

"Fuck. Do you have any idea what this does to me?" He watched her carefully, gauging her responses.

She placed her hand over his throbbing cock. "I have some idea."

He stepped back. "Are you trying to test my control?" He took rejuvenating breaths, fighting the urge to rip her skirt from her hips and fuck her the way they both needed it. He fisted his hands, struggling for control.

"I would never do that," she whispered softly, the teasing lilt in her voice enough to make any sane man crazy.

"Take it off," he said through clenched teeth. "Take it off and show me your pussy. Let me see how bad you need it."

In a move that had sweet submissive written all over her, she lowered her head, slipped her hand around her back and tugged on her zipper. He listened to the hiss, his eyes devouring her as she wiggled her skirt to her feet. She stepped out of it and stood before him completely naked.

He shoved a foot between her ankles. "Open your legs."

She spread for him, and he took in her shaved pussy. Her nether lips opened to expose her pretty pink sweetness. He sucked in air, lust calling out his Dom again. Christ, his depth of desire for her was beyond his comprehension. As he hungered for her, he took in another quick breath to force oxygen into his brain.

In a move that took him by surprise, she dropped to her knees before him.

"Rebecca," he rasped, reaching around to cup the back of her head. "What are you doing?"

Instead of answering, she opened his pants and drew his cock into her hot mouth. When her heat wrapped around his girth he gripped her hair, wrapping it around his hand three times. She sucked deep and he growled. Jesus, how could he do things the way she normally would when she was on her knees in front of him like this?

He tugged on her hair, hard, dragging her mouth from his cock. Her lips fell closed as her eyes flashed to his.

"Open," he commanded.

Responding to his authority, she widened her mouth. He moved his hips, offering her his crown only. She greedily licked him, and when she tried to draw him deeper into her throat, he pulled out. A popping sound filled the air as she sat before him, her mouth forming a sexy O as she waited. He let her wait, let her come to terms with the fact that no matter how hard she tried there was no way to suppress her submissive side.

"Please," she begged, leaving no question about what she wanted from him.

"Open wider."

She obliged and let him take charge as he fed her another inch. He took a breath to center himself, but the sight of her swollen lips sliding over his cock damn near did him in. Ravishing her mouth, he sank deeper until he touched the back of her throat, then withdrew, repeating the action until he was so goddamn stiff there was no longer any blood in his brain.

She moaned and sucked hard, then put her hands on her knees. Did she even realize what she was doing? Perhaps her actions were a result of being back in his room, a place where he'd first used restraints on her. He wasn't sure, but what he did know was that there was a deeper part of her that needed submission. The Dom in him responded, wanting to fulfill all her wants and desires.

The second he realized they were both fighting a losing battle, all coherent thought fled. A growl tore from his throat and with little finesse he pulled her to her feet and gave a shove until she was sprawled out on his bed. Need twisted inside him as she looked up at him, the passion and want in her eyes touching him on a completely different level. She licked her bottom lip, then lowered her eyes, her chest rising and falling as her cheeks turned a pretty shade of pink.

"On your knees."

She turned, and a noise sounded in her throat as she went up on her hands and knees, her sweet ass aimed his way. As she offered herself up so nicely, he removed his clothes, slid in behind her and gripped his cock. He smacked the length of his dick against her cheeks, then ran it between her legs, biting back a growl as he brushed the wet tip over her damp opening.

His pre-come glistened on her cheeks, and she wiggled her ass. Before he could think better of it, he slapped her backside. "Stop it," he said.

She whimpered, and her hands fisted the bedding. Quinn grabbed a pillow and stuffed it under her stomach, then pressed on her back until she collapsed onto it. Her hands stretched out over her head, and Quinn slipped a finger beneath her, running it over her wet clit. She pushed against it, grinding herself against him as she trapped his hand between her body and the pillow.

Jesus, he loved the way she reacted to him, how much she wanted him. He slapped her ass again. "Stop moving."

She stilled and he brushed her clit harder, rewarding her for her compliance. "That's it," he said. "Just lie still and let me take care of you the way you need."

He ran one hand over her soft backside and pulled his finger from her clit to slip it inside her. Her muscles clenched, and a storm built inside him. As his body trembled, the need to possess consumed him.

His cock throbbed, urging him to drive inside and claim her. He blinked, a red-hot blur of need making his vision fuzzy. He worked his finger between her legs, stroking the bundle of nerves inside until she trembled beneath him. She grew slicker with each stroke, and a slow burn worked its way through his body, settling deep in his groin. Her sweet scent urged him on and he turned his attention back to her clit. He teased it, changing the pressure and alternating between hard and fast, light and soft. As her orgasm approached, she quivered beneath his ministrations and stopped breathing. A moment passed and she continued to hold her breath. Jesus Christ, she was waiting for his command. Did she even realize that?

"Come for me, kitten," he said. He ran the rough pad of his finger over her clit, touching her just the way she liked, and her entire body shook. Her sweet cream coated his fingers, and for one brief, luxurious moment he pictured her tied to the St.

Andrew's cross, in nothing but the red bra and panties he'd sent to her office.

He shook his head to clear it and with renewed purpose grabbed her ass cheeks and squeezed. His fingers bit into her flesh as he pulled her open and positioned his cock at her hot pussy. He waited, building the anticipation inside her, and when a whimpering noise sounded in her throat he slapped her ass and plunged deep.

Heaven.

Pure fucking heaven.

A moment passed as he reveled in her wet heat, then he pulled out only to ram back inside again. He leaned over her and absorbed the tremors in her body as he took her higher and higher again. Senses heightened, his cock twitched and jerked as it filled with heated blood. His seed raced to the finish line but he struggled to hang on, never wanting to leave the warmth of her body. But the second he felt her climax around him, he knew he was beyond the point of no return.

He buried himself deep and exploded inside her, giving over to his body's needs.

So good. So fucking good. He stayed like that for a long moment, moisture sealing their bodies together. He breathed against her back and drew her scent into his lungs as one hand went to her hair to pull it from her face, needing to see her.

By small degrees he pulled out, his heart settling back to a steady rhythm. He dragged the pillow out from underneath her, then rolled to his back. He drew her to him and wrapped a protective arm around her. She snuggled in and he shifted to face her.

"Rebecca," he began. Shit, he really should apologize for slipping into the role that came so natural to him, but how could he when he knew it was so good for her. Her stomach took that moment to grumble and she crinkled her nose, lifting her chin until their eyes met.

Contentment backlit her eyes and told him so much about her needs. She wanted his dominance every bit as much as he wanted her submission.

"I went to Sophie's party straight from work and only had a few hor d'oeuvres," she explained.

He smiled, dropped a soft kiss onto her mouth and said, "Let's get you something to eat." She was about to move when he stopped her. "Wait. Why don't you stay here?"

She gave him a teasing look. "Are you afraid that now that I got what I wanted from you, I'm going to leave?"

"Yeah, something like that," he said, chuckling as he pulled on a pair of jeans. He drew up his zipper, then stilled, sensing there was more to that statement, a deeper meaning. Did she expect him to leave once he'd gotten what he wanted? Did that kind of thing happen to her often? Knowing now was not the right time to probe, he said, "But just remember, there's more where that came from."

She snuggled deeper into the blankets. "Hurry back."

He glanced at the clock then left the room, moving quietly down the hall. The staff had already gone to bed, so he hurried to the kitchen and pulled open the fridge. He grinned when he saw the tray of sandwiches inside. He'd have to remember to give

Eloise a raise. He grabbed the tray, two glasses from the rack, and a bottle of white wine.

By the time he made it back to his room, he found Rebecca with her back pressed against the headboard, thumbing through an old photo album. She glanced up when he entered.

"I hope you don't mind."

"My house is your house." He poured them each a glass of wine, then set the bottle and sandwiches on his nightstand. He handed her one and she munched as she flipped through the pages. The smile on her face warmed his heart.

He took a big bite of his ham and Swiss and pointed to his brother Gabe. "He's the baby of the family. Momma's boy all the way. We couldn't do anything wrong without him tattling."

She laughed. "I don't know about that. I think you were all momma's boys." She chewed her sandwich and went quiet for a moment. "What was it like growing up in a big family?"

Quinn took a sip of his wine. "For us kids it was great, but how my mother put up with four boys and a husband was beyond me. We weren't exactly angels."

"No?"

He laughed. "Hell no. Josh and I had a misguided youth, but Dad's belt got us back on track."

She chuckled. "Is your dad…?" Her question trailed off, as if she didn't want to dig too deep.

"He died a few years back. He was a good man."

"And you're close with all your brothers."

"Thick as thieves."

She laughed. "Gabe doesn't tattle anymore?"

"No. We have too much on him these days for that."

They ate their sandwiches as she flipped through a few more pages, a look of longing on her face. She finished her wine and he took the glass. "Do you have any more albums?" she asked.

"Yeah." He climbed from the bed and searched his bookshelf. By the time he found one, he turned to find her sound asleep.

His heart squeezed to see her so warm and content in his bed. He put the book back, slid in beside her and tucked her in. In no time at all he fell asleep. A sound pulled him awake, and he turned, half expecting her to be gone after realizing they had indeed crossed over into BDSM last night. When he found her still sleeping quietly, the love he felt for her tightened his throat. A noise sounded again, and Quinn climbed from the bed and pulled on his jeans.

He tiptoed down the hall and found his brother coming in through the front door.

"Hey," Quinn said. "Early morning?"

Josh grinned. "More like late night."

From the kitchen, he spotted Eloise preparing coffee. "We'll take it in the den," he said.

Josh followed him in and sat on the edge of his desk. "How are…things?" he asked.

"I don't know. She's giving me mixed signals and I don't even think she knows it. I want to give her what she wants but she's not ready."

"She's afraid."

Quinn opened the box with the collar and ran his fingers over the jewels. It symbolized a commitment to each other, as well as the BDSM lifestyle. How would she react if she knew he'd had it made for her?

Eloise brought their coffee and they both sipped in silence until she left. "I know you care about her, bro, but is giving up a big part of who you are what you want to do? If she loved you in return, would she really ask for that?"

"She didn't. I offered. She refused. I insisted." Quinn scrubbed his hand over the scruff on his chin. "I want to be what she needs. Even if we stayed in the lifestyle, there is still a piece of herself she won't give to me, anyway, which means I could never collar her."

"Then why don't you move back to L.A. with me. Start again."

His office door creaked, and he looked up, expecting to see Eloise. When he spotted Rebecca standing there in one of his robes his heart missed a beat. Her gaze left his and went to the collar in the box. He quickly closed it. Shit, how much of their conversation had she overheard?

He crossed the room to her and that's when he noticed the glazed look in her eyes. He waved his hand in front of her face. "Rebecca," he said.

"What?" she asked, her gaze moving over his face.

"Where'd you go?"

She blinked and squared her shoulders. "I have to go," she said. "I need to go home and get ready for work."

"It's Saturday."

She gave him a forced smile. "I'm a workaholic, remember."

Quinn looked at the clock. "Okay," he whispered, taking her hand in his and leading her back to the bedroom. "Let's get dressed. But before I drop you off at home, there is somewhere I'd like to take you." He cupped her face and looked deep into her eyes. What he was about to do next would either solidify their relationship or rip it wide open. But no matter what happened to them, he had to do this—for her.

Seven

Rebecca sat in the vehicle beside Quinn and kept glancing his way. She took in his strong profile as he maneuvered his sports car through the early morning weekend traffic. He kept his focus on the road straight ahead. Was he avoiding direct eye contact with her on purpose? Perhaps he was worried about what she'd overheard in his den.

Her mind returned to the conversation between him and his brother, and the beautiful diamond-studded collar he'd had made for her. Her heart tightened because she knew what that collar represented— complete physical and mental surrender.

That idea squeezed the air from her lungs and told her one thing. Today, after he dropped her off, she was going to end it with him, no matter how hard it would be to not have him in her life. He deserved a woman who could give him all parts of herself, and she couldn't do that.

She glanced out the window and an uneasy feeling gripped her when he started into the neighborhood she was far too familiar with. Surely to God he wasn't…

He rounded the corner and reached for her hand, giving it a reassuring squeeze.

"Quinn?" She sat up a little straighter in her seat, the hairs on the back of her neck prickling. "Where are we going?"

"Almost there," he said, shooting her a quick look. The car slowed outside Dorothy Kean's home, and her gaze locked with his. Fight or flight instincts kicked in and urged her to flee, to get as far away from the place as possible.

She pulled her hand from his. "What the hell do you think you're doing?" She gripped her forehead, pushing her hair from her face as she tried to wrap her brain around this unexpected turn of events. Quinn reached for her hand again and she snatched it back, anger coming sure and swift. "You shouldn't have brought me here. Take me home right now."

"Rebecca," he said, his voice soft. "Just hear me out."

The car seemed to be closing in on her, choking the last of the air from her lungs. She could feel Quinn's eyes assessing her. She turned from him and glanced at the house. A gasp caught in her throat when she saw Dorothy exiting the front door and making her way down the weed-infested walkway. She walked down the cracked and pitted sidewalk with a cane, hobbling past the car without noticing Rebecca inside. Rebecca's stomach twisted and she gripped the dash to steady herself.

"She can't hurt you anymore," Quinn said quietly. "Look at her, she's nothing but a lonely old lady lost in her own misery."

"How…how do you know her?"

"I paid her a visit."

"You did? Why?"

"I wanted to try to figure out what happened to you."

He had no right to do this. Panic gripped her. "She knows who you are?"

"No. I made up a story about a neighborhood watch program."

The hem of Dorothy's dress swayed as she walked away and Rebecca's heart slammed harder against her chest.

"Just look at her," Quinn said again. "She'll never hurt you again. No one will. Because I'll never let them." Rebecca had spent so many years hating the woman—fearing her. "She's old and broken and not the least bit scary."

Rebecca took in her feeble and twisted frame. Quinn was right. She didn't seem so scary anymore. Didn't look like the monster she remembered from her youth. Not only did she look old and frail, she looked completely alone and miserable. It almost made Rebecca feel sorry for her. Almost.

She turned to Quinn and didn't realize he had her hand in his. "Why did you bring me here?" she asked again.

"To confront old ghosts."

"You had no right to do this." She shook her head. "I told you something private and you betrayed me."

"You must know by now how much I care about you, Rebecca. How I would do anything for you."

She looked at her lap. "I can't give you what you want, and you shouldn't change for me."

"I'm not asking for anything more than for you to face your past. These things inside you…you need to confront them before you can let them go."

She opened her mouth to demand he take her home, but he pressed his fingers to her lips. "This house…your youth, has something to do with being afraid of the dark. I want to help you move past that."

She scoffed. "Why? So you can have me the way you want me in the bedroom?" she shot back. "Jesus, Quinn. You should have just left me alone after our trip to the resort."

"This isn't about me, Rebecca. This is about being free, period. From a childhood riddled with uncertainty and rejection. From the darkness forced upon you by a cruel and unloving woman. About recognizing your inner strength and overcoming your fears of darkness and embracing the security and pleasures that it offers. I'll be with you all the way, but that first step is yours to take."

"How do you know all this? I never told you where I grew up."

"I had a friend look into it."

With her emotions running high, tears filled her eyes. "You had no right."

"I know, and I'm sorry. I took what you told me in private and dug deeper. I hope at some point you realize I did it for you, to help you free yourself."

She shook her head. "You have no idea what you're talking about."

"Okay, then prove me wrong. Come inside with me." He opened his door, crossed in front of the car and came around to her side.

With defiance urging her on, she put her hand on the door handle, then hesitated as old memories resurfaced. Her glance met Quinn's, and when she saw the reassurance in his eyes, strength blossomed inside her and her chin came up. He was right. The things that had happened in that house were still controlling her, robbing her of having normalcy in her life, her relationships, and no matter how scary, it was time to face her demons, slay them, and put them behind her once and for all. She gave a small tug on the door handle. The second it opened, Quinn was there beside her, his arm around her waist.

He held her as they crossed the street and climbed the stairs. She hesitated again. "Dorothy isn't even in there for me to confront."

"That doesn't mean we can't go in." He pulled a credit card from his back pocket and slipped it between the door and the frame.

She gasped. "What are you doing?"

"Opening the door. These locks are as old as Dorothy, easy to pick."

"How do you know how to do that?"

"Misguided youth, remember?'"

"This is breaking and entering."

"Don't worry. I'll take all the blame."

She stepped back. "I'm a lawyer, Quinn."

"Good. If I get caught you can get me off."

The door opened and when she caught the smell of pine cleanser, old memories hit again. Her stomach twisted, bile pushing into her throat. "I hated it here, Quinn. When I left I swore I'd never look back." She stepped away, but Quinn took her hand. It was a small thing, so often taken for granted, but that touch, his presence, his support helped her go on.

"Sweetheart, you can't move forward until you look back. You have things you need to deal with and overcome."

He stepped inside and she hesitated. She looked over her shoulder to see a car turn the corner. Not wanting to get caught hovering on the doorstep like a convict, she darted inside, shut the door behind her and leaned against it.

The second she saw the door to the basement, she became overwhelmed with anxiety. Panic gripped hard and she clutched her chest. A noise sounded in the kitchen and she nearly jumped out of her skin.

"It's just the cat," Quinn said.

She nodded and noted the way he was watching her with great care, the way he always watched her.

She looked at the basement door again and pinched her eyes shut, her mind going back to when she was thirteen. She was so angry when she'd first come to live here. She'd been so good at the previous home— did her homework, washed the dishes, and always did as she was told. When those foster parents tossed her aside when she hit her teen years, it left a bitter taste in her mouth and a huge hole in her heart. She'd acted out here at first, but had quickly learned that her disobedience came with severe punishment.

Her gaze went to the heavy lock dangling on the loop, and under her breath she said, "It's still there."

Quinn turned and followed the direction of her gaze. He stepped away and touched the lock. "This?" he asked.

She nodded, unable to get the words past the lump in her throat.

"What happened here?" he asked, his voice soft.

She swallowed and managed to get out, "I don't like the dark."

He pointed to the cellar. "She put you down there, didn't she?"

She didn't need to answer. Her shaking body said it all.

"I'm going down," Quinn said.

Her hand darted out and she grabbed him. "Don't. It's full of rats and God knows what else."

"I'm not afraid of rats."

"I am." A sob caught in her throat as she recalled the sounds of the rats closing in on her. She brushed at her clothes and hugged herself. It took all her mental strength not to lose it back then. Rebecca glanced at the front door, then back at Quinn. "What if she comes back?"

He held the lock out in his palm, then squeezed it. "She can't hurt you anymore. Not if you don't let her." Quinn reached up and pulled a chain dangling from the ceiling—one she could never reach as a kid—and the light to the basement flicked on.

She took a tentative step forward and squeezed his hand hard as he led her to the dank, musty basement, the smells instantly taking her back in time. Her heels clicked on the cement floors when they reached the bottom, and she looked around. Besides the washer and dryer there was nothing in the basement, nothing for her to be afraid of.

Her ears perked at the squeaking sounds, and she practically jumped into Quinn's arms. "I can hear them," she cried out.

He cupped her face. "Rebecca, sweetheart, what you hear are the pipes. This place is old. There are no rats down here, nothing at all to hurt you." He waved his hand. "Look around, and when you realize that it's not scary in the light of day, you'll know you have nothing to fear in the dark of night."

She brushed her clothes again. "I could feel them. They were trying to bite me."

"Here." He lifted her hand and held it over a vent. "This is what you probably felt. You were a child, and in the dark, the mind can turn anything into a monster."

"She told me one of these days the rats would eat me alive. I lived in fear. I used to curl up and recite the alphabet, just to help me focus on something else."

Emotions flashed in Quinn's eyes. He pulled her to him and hugged her. "You were young, afraid, an innocent thirteen-year-old child who believed her because she was an adult. And adults are supposed to do what's best, right?" She nodded and he continued, "But she let you down, Rebecca. She didn't protect you the way she was supposed to."

She blinked at him. "I told on her once when some ladies came to check on me, but they didn't believe me. The punishment was worse after that." She sniffed back the tears that were falling harder now. "I was scared of her. Too scared to ever tell again, because I didn't know what she'd do to me."

"I know, and I can promise you this. I will never let anything happen to you again."

"I want to go now."

He nodded and led her back up the stairs. When they reached the top, the front door opened and in walked Dorothy. Her eyes went wide and she dropped the small grocery bag. "What are you doing in my home?" she asked, her voice frantic, brittle. Arthritic, gnarled hands lifted the cane and pointed it at them. "Get out right now or you'll be sorry."

Rebecca straightened. "You don't scare me anymore."

Her eyes narrowed. "Rebecca?"

"Yeah, it's me."

She stumbled backward. "I…I…"

"You what?"

"I did it for your own good."

A strangled sound rose from Rebecca's throat. "What's done is done, but the only one you have to make it right with now is your maker. Now step out of the way, we're leaving."

Dorothy hobbled to the living room and the second Rebecca stepped outside, she took a big breath and let it out slowly, releasing all the pain and fear she'd had bottled up inside her for so long. Her legs weakened and she gripped the rail.

Quinn held her. "I got you."

She took in the fierceness in his eyes, along with his vow to protect her, but he'd betrayed her trust by taking her here and now things would never be the same between them.

"I want to go home."

Quinn guided her to his vehicle, and after seeing her into the passenger seat, he slid in beside her and turned the engine over. Twenty minutes later, she was climbing out onto the sidewalk outside her condo. Quinn slipped the stick into park and joined her.

His hand closed over hers and he dropped a kiss onto her forehead. Everything in the way he touched her, looked at her, shattered her last vestige of control. After everything she'd been though with Quinn, Felix and seeing that old house again, she'd never be that same Rebecca again.

"I want to be alone," she said.

"I'm not leaving you, Rebecca. I'm never leaving you."

She touched his face, needing time to sort through everything she'd been through. "Please, Quinn. I just need time to myself. There are things I need to sort through."

He squeezed his eye shut. "Can I at least come in? I'll stay in another room and give you space."

"No." He was about to protest again, but she stopped him. "I need to be away from you."

Jesus. "How far away?"

"Quinn—"

"Just tell me what you need, Rebecca. I'll do whatever you want. If you want me to move to L.A. with my brother because being here is too near, then I'll do it, but I need to know you're okay."

"What I need is to be alone," she said and walked away.

He shook his head, and even though it went against his protective nature, he turned from her. "I'm only a call away. I'll be here in seconds if you need me."

She nodded, needing quiet time, because she'd never dealt with these kinds of emotions before. "I know."

He stayed in his car until she was safely inside her condo, then she heard him roar away. Rebecca stripped off her clothes and made her way to the shower. She stayed under the hot spray for longer than normal, washing off the past—the stagnant smells of the old house, the dampness of the basement on her skin, the fear that paralyzed her. She squeezed her eyes shut, her mind sorting through everything that had happened since meeting Quinn.

Her heart raced when she thought about what he'd done for her, how he wanted to help her. And he *had* helped her by bringing warmth to her darkest corners as she confronted her past. She knew she'd never find in another what she'd found with him, and because of him, she was now a stronger, healthier Rebecca. Body and mind.

She felt a deep, needy ache in her core. Her whole life everyone had left her. But Quinn hadn't. In fact, he stayed with her even when she couldn't give him what he deserved. She let loose a breath, and for the first time in her life she wasn't afraid of getting close, wasn't afraid of letting down her guard. Deep in her heart she knew Quinn was never going to walk away or discard her like she was yesterday's news.

He'd taken a risk by betraying her trust and was willing to lose her to help her. She ran through the series of events that led her to this place, this revelation. Her heart fluttered. It was worth everything they'd been through to get to this moment.

Quinn had tried so hard to change, to give up the one thing that drew her to him in the first place. Earlier that morning after seeing the collar and knowing it represented a lifestyle she was running away from, she'd decided to walk away from Quinn, because he deserved better.

A laugh lodged in her throat, because honest to God, it would be easier to give up breathing than to quit him. He was an incredible man who had taught her so much about herself, and now... Well, now everything was different.

She climbed from the shower, wrapped in a towel and made her way into the kitchen to make a cup of tea. Her mind went back to the gorgeous diamond-encrusted collar, and this time she felt a little thrill to know what he was asking of her. BDSM was all about trust, and she knew before she could wear it she'd have to surrender herself to Quinn, physically and *mentally*. That might have scared her before, but she believed in Quinn, trusted him with her body and her mind. She glanced at her phone as an idea began to formulate. Oh yeah, she knew just what she had to do to show him how much she trusted him, how committed she was to making this right between them—before it was too late.

Eight

"Forget it, Josh. You'll have to find your own way to the resort. I'm not stepping foot on the island. Never again."

"You don't have to. I'm just asking for a lift, that's all. You don't even have to get out of the plane. Just drop me off and turn around."

Jesus, why did he have such a hard time saying no to his twin. "You checked all the other charters?"

"Every one of them. There's nothing available."

"You have to go tonight?"

"It's Saturday night. Come on. All you're doing is moping around here anyway."

Quinn looked at his watch. It had been hours since he left Rebecca and he was still waiting to hear from her.

"She already texted to say she was going to sleep. You're not going to hear from her now. Besides, I talked to Sophie earlier, and she was on her way to Rebecca's place. She's in good hands, don't worry."

"Fine." Quinn grabbed his phone off his desk and shoved it into his pocket. "Let's go." They climbed into Quinn's car and a few hours later they were buckled in his Cessna and on the way to the resort. Quinn remained relatively quiet, worried about Rebecca. Had he pushed her to far? Pushed her right out of his life? He could deal with that, if it meant he'd helped her. But goddammit, he needed to hear from her more than he needed his next breath.

He shot a glance at Josh, who seemed out of sorts. "What's wrong?" he asked.

"Oh, nothing. I just haven't been here in a while. I'm probably going to need you to sign me in."

"I told you, I'm not staying."

"Come on, big brother," Josh said, and Quinn rolled his eyes. Josh only played into the big brother thing when he wanted something. "What if you turn around and they close the doors on me. Just sign me in, that's all I'm asking."

"Fine, then I'm leaving. And you can have these too. I no longer need them." He fished his cabana keys from his pocket and handed them over. "It's yours."

"You're giving it to me."

"Sure. I told you. I'm leaving this behind."

Quinn circled the small island. Nighttime was upon them when he landed the plane on the small runway and powered it down.

He unlatched his seatbelt and followed his brother to the small airport, where they took a shuttle to the castle. The place was quiet, not a member to be found. Quinn looked at his watch as he climbed the steps.

"What's going on? This place should be in full swing by now." He tried the door and found it locked. He frowned. Had Alexander shut the place down? He turned to look out over the island and the key to the castle jingled in his pocket. He grabbed it and opened the door to find Jacob standing there. What the hell?

"What's going on?" Quinn asked, taking in the almost amused look on the man's face. His glance went to his brother, and when he found him smirking, Quinn squared his shoulders. "Josh?" he asked, a warning in his voice. He started to back away. "I don't know what you're up to but if you think bringing me here is going to—"

"You're going to need this," Josh said, handing his cabana key back.

"Right this way," Jacob said, waving his hand toward the hall. "Your submissive awaits."

Quinn's heart started pounding, hitting his ribcage so hard it was ringing in his ears. "I don't want a submissive. I'm with Rebecca."

Josh gave him a little shove. "Just trust me on this."

"Josh—"

"Come on, big brother."

Josh pushed him down the hall, and Quinn fought against him. "So help me, you better not have set me up with someone to prove I can't quit the lifestyle. The only one I want is Rebecca."

"Just keep going," Josh said.

They stopped walking when they reached his favorite playroom. Jacob waved his hand. "Your sub awaits," he said, then stood beside Josh.

Quinn looked into the room and what he saw next was like a physical blow to the stomach. He grabbed the doorframe for support and briefly pinched his eyes shut, expecting the vision to be gone when he opened them again.

He blinked, the beautiful sight of Rebecca tied to the cross, dressed in the red silk panties and bra he'd sent her, with a blindfold on her eyes, nearly made him sob. She'd set this up. For him.

He searched for his voice. "Rebecca," he said, stepping up to her. He removed the blindfold, pushing it to her forehead. "You don't have to do this," he said, finding it harder and harder to breathe. "Not for me."

Her face was full of warmth and admiration, trust and respect as she looked at him. "I know I don't have to, but I want to."

His heart hurt so bad it made it difficult to talk. "Rebecca, no you don't need to do this. I know what happened in bed last night, but I can quit this, I promise. You don't need to change for me. I'll change for you."

"This isn't about me changing to be who you need me to be. This is who I am, Quinn. Just like you've been trying to be the man I needed. But all along you *were* the man I needed. Just the way you were."

He cupped her face and gazed into her eyes. When he saw love shining there, everything he felt for her rocketed through him. Was this happening? Was this really happening?

He pressed his forehead to hers. "I was so scared I'd lost you."

"You're not getting rid of me so easily."

"I want you, Rebecca, forever."

"I know." She made a gesture with her head and he turned to see the collar sitting on a chair. The world went out from underneath him.

His heart thundered and his voice was rough with emotions when he said, "Tell me how much you want this…want me."

"I want this, and I want you," she answered, her expression filled with pure admiration.

He touched the slip of red silk covering her hips, and when he caught the sweet tang of her arousal, possession raced through him. He crossed the room, came back with the collar. "You're mine, Rebecca," he said, putting the collar around her neck and clasping it from behind. "Every part of you."

"Every part of me is yours, Quinn. Yours to keep."

Thank you!

Thank you so much for reading, YOURS: Billionaire CEO Romance Series. I hope you enjoyed all the stories as much as I loved writing them. If you loved boxed sets, check out Firefighter Heat, and Stone Cliff Series! Keep reading for an excerpt from FEVER, Firefighter Heat.

Interested in leaving a review? Please do! Reviews help readers connect with books that work for them. I appreciate all reviews, whether positive or negative.

Happy Reading,
Cathryn

Fever Excerpt

One

Strawberry daiquiri in hand, Sara Jack blew a wispy auburn curl off her forehead and glanced around *The Hose,* her reporter's eye stopping to examine the men crowded around the pool table. She studied them for a long moment, as though the sight of their scrumptious backsides was actually newsworthy. Of course, back in Trenton, Iowa, aka, Butthole Nowhere, such a sight really *was* newsworthy. But here in Chicago, tight firefighter buns were a dime a dozen, she supposed. And damned if she didn't want to grab herself the *baker's* special, to go. Thirteen fresh, warm honey buns.

Mmmmm…yummy.

She sipped her fruity drink and considered the name of the establishment again. *The Hose*, she mused. What a perfectly delicious name to describe the local watering hole where the firefighters from station 419 gathered nightly for a game of eight ball.

As Sara blocked out the din of the crowd, and completely ignored the bridal party members lounging around the table beside her, her lascivious gaze panned the hotties in the room a second time. Her investigative eyes zeroed in on one very sexy, very "well-equipped" Mitch Adams as he turned in her direction. The man had been warming her blood and getting under her skin during their rehearsals without even trying.

As she devoured his broad shoulders, his firm stomach, and his even firmer thighs, a slow heat gravitated south and burned her body from the inside out. She licked her suddenly parched lips, her mind wandering, conjuring up all the wicked ways Mitch, with his lethally honed physique and panty-soaking smile, could help extinguish those slow burning embers.

The Hose, she mused again, her glance settling a few inches below Mitch's leather belt. What a great name for the firefighters' bar - a name, she suspected, or at least hoped, had nothing to do with their profession.

Beer in one hand, pool cue in the other, Mitch lazily crossed his legs at the ankles and leaned against the pool table. Dark hair cut short gave him a charming boy-next-door look, but Sara suspected he was anything but.

Unlike the "nice boys" she'd dated back home, pleasant, spineless boys who bored her to death - inside the bedroom and out - Mitch had a raw sexuality about him that screamed of sex, sin and...*danger*. Sara shivered. Almost violently. Surprised at just how much his carnal edginess aroused her.

Her gaze brushed over him again, taking pleasure in his square jaw, perfect white teeth, long athletic body, and bad-boy attitude. Sexual awareness prowled through her, warming her blood. Her glance traveled onward and upward until she met with a set of bedroom blues that shimmered with dark desire when they locked on hers. Mitch shot her a look that held all kinds of suggestions, all kinds of wicked possibilities.

Sara drew a sharp breath, her pulse pounding in her throat. She wiped her hands on her snug jeans, letting the denim drink in her moisture.

As he watched her watching him, his nostrils flared and his body tensed, tension lines bracketing his sensuous mouth. In that brief moment when their gazes collided, they shared a heated exchange, one that could undoubtedly set the crowded establishment ablaze.

It occurred to Sara that she wasn't the only woman in the bar taken by his edgy sexuality. She twisted sideways, noting the way the other women in the room watched him, their body language indicating they'd like a tour of his station, with up- close and personal instructions on how he handled his hose.

Just then, Cassie Williams, the beautiful bride-to-be, the same woman who was responsible for Sara's unexpected trip to Chicago, stepped up to the table. Sara welcomed the distraction and shifted in the chair to face her.

Sara had been best friends with Cassie since kindergarten, which was why she, along with her other best friends, Jenna Powers and Megan Wagner, had dropped everything and hopped on the first plane to Chicago. Nothing short of a category-five catastrophe would keep them all from attending Cassie's nuptial exchange with sexy firefighter Nick Cameron.

With Sara's body still feeling the effects of Mitch's lusty gaze, she focused fully on Cassie.

"Pretty cute, isn't he?" Cassie asked with a knowing look on her face as she gestured toward Mitch with a nod.

"What? Who?" Sara asked, feigning innocence.

Ignoring her question, Cassie sat down and shimmied closer. She tapped Sara's nose. "Watch out for him, Sara. He's not like the nice boys you know from back home." Cassie remained quiet for a moment, while Sara mulled over that warning. A moment later, Cassie pitched her voice lower and added, "Mitch Adams is…dangerous."

"Dangerous?" Sara asked, her pulse racing a little faster, her internal temperature rising a little higher.

"Yeah, dangerous. A guy like that can capture your heart without even trying. And since I know you're a girl who wants commitment and doesn't want her heart broken, I suggest if you start anything with him, you go into it with your eyes wide open."

Eyes wide-open…legs wide-open. Oh, the possibilities.

"I've known Mitch long enough to know he's a no strings playboy, a woman's fantasy. It's the way he likes it."

Playboy. Fantasy. No strings. Sara wasn't seeing a downside here.

Cassie angled her head. "When you meet the right guy, you'll know it."

Sara shrugged one shoulder. "Maybe I'm not looking for the right guy." Honestly, she'd love to find Mr. Right and settle down. Not that she expected to find her *"knight in shining armor"* in a bad ass like Mitch. What she expected to find with him was a bad boy who was also so very, very good.

"He's a great guy to have fun with, but don't expect more, Cassie said. "I just don't want to see you hurt."

Sara worked to tamp down her desire and keep her voice even. Trying for casual she toyed with her straw and said, "How could he possibly hurt me? I'm here on a two-week vacation." She dragged her finger around the perimeter of her glass and continued, "From work and from reality." It suddenly occurred to her that a break from reality, along with a red hot fling with a *"dangerous,"* drop-dead-gorgeous firefighter, was just the thing she needed. What was that old vacation motto? What happened in Vegas stayed in Vegas. Surely that could apply to Chicago, too. Why couldn't she have a wild, no-strings-attached affair and live out a few firefighter fantasies of her own? At least then she'd have something to warm her thoughts when she returned home to Iowa, to her mundane fluff job as reporter for Trenton's small-time gazette.

The thoughts of going back to that office only to write another cow-tipping story made her shiver. Her dream job was to write sexy features for *Entice*, a young, hip, Chicago-based magazine for today's strong, sexually empowered women. The trick was to come up with a great, hot topic story, one that would impress the *Entice* editors. Unfortunately, hot-topic stories were few and far between in her small town.

Cassie's voice brought Sara's attention back around. "To him, women are just sperm banks."

Sara twisted her lips. "Sperm bank, huh?" It really had been far too long since she'd taken a deposit.

Sara looked over Cassie's shoulder and spotted Mitch watching their exchange with interest, giving her the impression he knew exactly what they were talking about. He scraped his hands over his chin, dragging her gaze to his fingertips.

Her heart beat in a mad rush as she thought about how those fingers would feel tracing the pattern of her body, and touching her most private areas. She pictured his mouth ravishing hers, his hands on her breasts, his thick cock ramming her pussy, fucking her like she'd never been fucked before.

Just then their eyes connected, and in that instant, Sara knew she'd like nothing better than to take a few deposits from the bad ass firefighter.

Someone from across the room called out to Mitch. He twisted sideways and followed the sound, vanishing from her line of sight.

Sara pulled in a fortifying breath and focused all her attention back on the girls, playing catch-up on their conversation, which, from the sounds of things, was just beginning to heat up.

Never one to be subtle, Megan got right to the point. "So tell me, Cassie. Is Nick any good in bed?"

Cassie kept a telltale grin from her face, but the fire in her eyes spoke volumes. "You know I don't kiss and tell."

"I'm not asking about his kissing abilities, I'm asking about his fu-"

"Jesus, Megan," Jenna piped in, "What kind of question is that?"

Megan shrugged. "I'm just asking, is all."

"What you really should be asking is, does he know his way around a vagina? Because the last guy I dated couldn't find my G-spot without a compass and detailed direction's from Google Maps."

A round of laughter erupted from the table and gained the attention of those around the four of them.

Still chuckling, Sara planted her elbow on the table and dropped her voice. "You think you've had it bad," she whispered, resting her chin on her palms. "My last date thought a G-spot was the crisp five dollar bill he handed the waitress every morning in exchange for his coffee and paper."

"Okay, since we're having a whose-boyfriend-thinks-a-vulva-is-something-they-drive-to-work-every-morning contest I want in," Megan added, laying her palms flat on the table, a wry grin curling her lips. "My ex-husband thought fellatio was something you ordered off the dessert menu at Applebee's." She smacked one hand to her forehead. "And to think I married him! What the fuck was I thinking?" A round of groans followed Megan's confession.

"Okay, you win," Sara piped in, going back to her drink. Maybe alcohol would lessen the painful truth that *all* the men back home were as boring in the bedroom as they were out of it.

Cassie leaned forward. She slipped something under her hand and slid it to the middle of the table. "Actually, there is a way you can all win. Except this time winning means *no* Google Maps, *no* detailed directions, and *no* Applebee's."

Before Cassie continued, her gaze darted around the room. Her voice dropped an octave as though all four women gathered around the table were masterminding some secret plan to take over the world. "This is just good, old-fashioned fun where those involved know what a G-spot is and how to work it."

The other women all huddled forward, mimicking Cassie's actions.

Megan lowered her voice to match Cassie's. "What are you talking about?"

Cassie lifted her hand from the table to reveal a small white business card. A hush fell over the group as all sets of eyes focused on the rectangular piece of cardboard.

After a long moment, Jenna broke the silence. "The Hot Line?" She crinkled her nose, her glance going from the card to Cassie, then back to the card again. "What the hell is The Hot Line?"

With a fairly good idea of what Cassie was suggesting, Sara scooped the card up for a better look. It simply read, The Hot Line, with a phone number, 555-HEAT.

Sara shot Cassie a look, her mind racing with indecent ideas. She furrowed her brow, the reporter in her needing clarification, the woman in her blazing to life. "Yeah, what the hell is the Hot Line, Cassie?" she asked, examining the card.

"It's a way for you all to have a little fun, with men who know their way around a woman's body."

"Oh yeah?" Megan rushed out, eyes bright with excitement. "Enlighten me, chicky."

Cassie tapped the card, which Sara continued to clutch like her life depended on it. Okay, so maybe her *life* didn't depend on it, but her libido sure as hell did.

Cassie got right to the point. "If you call The Hot Line and mention that you need assistance, it will bring a sexy firefighter – a sexy 'fully equipped' firefighter, that is – to your door, ready and willing to tamp down your fires."

"Damn girl, give me that card!" Megan flashed a wide smile. Mischief danced in her eyes as she whipped the card out of Sara's hands.

Pussy clenching in anticipation, Sara snatched the card back, the investigative side of her demanding proof. "Is this for real?"

Cassie's hand closed over hers and squeezed. "Absolutely. How do you think I met Nick?" There was honesty in her eyes when she spoke, and nothing in her voice to suggest otherwise. "It's also a very well-kept secret." She grew quiet for a moment and then said, "I trust you know what to do with it."

Suddenly Sara's entire body went on high alert. She knew Mitch was standing behind her, felt him long before she saw him. His heat reached out to her, his scent closing around her like warm blanket. She inhaled, pulling his spicy aroma into her lungs, noting the way her body stirred to life whenever he was near. Lust burned through her, and her mind sifted through all the ways Mitch could help stoke that fire.

Mitch leaned over her shoulder and grabbed a handful of nuts. Sara drew a shaky breath, cream pooling between her legs. She closed her hand over the card, and angled her body to face him. The sight of him up close and personal had her libido reacting with urgent demands, clamoring for his undivided attention. His bad-boy smile did delicious things to her insides. Her body flushed, immediately. The man made her feel so edgy, so out of control, so fucking hot.

In a hushed tone, he spoke to her, and her alone. "I have to take off. I'll be at the firehouse." His voice was low, deeply intimate. His sexy tenor curled around her, her nipples tightening in response. As sexual tension whipped between them, basic elemental need took hold. Her mouth salivated, and her pussy ached to slide down his pole and ride him with wild abandonment.

A round of "G'nights" followed a path around the table as he prepared to leave.

Before Mitch stepped away, he cast Sara a suggestive look and touched her shoulder, his knuckles brushing her cheek in a gentle caress that stimulated all her nerve endings. Something compelled her to touch him in return. When her fingers closed over his, it brought passion to his blue eyes. His dark, seductive gaze told her that not only could he fuck her, and fuck her good, but he could also make all her fantasies come true. His glance went to her other hand, the one covering the card.

Did he know what she had hidden under there?

He paused for a moment, as though weighing his words carefully. Then, with his expression tender and hot, he whispered to her in the deepest, sexiest tone, "*Later*," and disappeared into the crowd.

Holy. Shit. That one word, combined with everything in his voice and everything in his manner, spoke volumes and had her aching to discover the truth behind the Hot Line.

Did these firefighters risk their lives daily to put out dangerous fires, save little kittens from trees, and rescue libidinous women? She took a moment to entertain the idea. If she dialed the number, would a very sexy, very "well-equipped" Mitch Adams show up at her door and help tamp down the flames of desire engulfing her?

She swallowed. Hard.

Her mind raced, the reporter in her perking up. With casual aplomb, she scooped up the card and slipped it into her pocket, realizing that if the Hot Line really did exist, she'd just been presented with the perfect opportunity to write a hot- topic story. And if she gave it her own sexy spin, it could be just the article she needed to launch her career at *Entice*.

She looked up in time to see Mitch slip out the door. The scrumptious sight of his tight backside made her shiver with longing. She drew a centering breath, and worked to push back the rising lust.

As her fingers toyed with the edge of the card, her mind filled with wild and wicked ideas. Naturally, like any good reporter, she'd have to do a little investigative research of her own before she wrote the article. And in the process, she planned on exploring a few firefighter fantasies along the way.

About Cathryn Fox

New York Times and *USA Today* best selling author, Cathryn is a wife, mom, sister, daughter, and friend. She loves dogs, sunny weather, anything chocolate (she never says no to a brownie) pizza and red wine. She has two teenagers who keep her busy with their never ending activities, and a husband who is convinced he can turn her into a mixed martial arts fan. Cathryn can never find balance in her life, is always trying to find time to go to the gym, can never keep up with emails, Facebook or Twitter and tries to write page-turning books that her readers will love.

Connect with Cathryn:
Tsu: https://www.tsu.co/CathrynFox
Newsletter:
https://app.mailerlite.com/webforms/landing
/c1f8n1
Twitter: https://twitter.com/writercatfox

Facebook:
https://www.facebook.com/AuthorCathrynF
ox?ref=hl
Blog: http://cathrynfox.com/blog/
Goodreads:
https://www.goodreads.com/author/show/91
799.Cathryn_Fox
Pinterest
http://www.pinterest.com/catkalen/